MISTLETOES AND HOOD LOVE WITH A BOW

Tessa J

are intended to give the novel a sense of reality. Any similarity in other names, characters, places, and incidents are entirely coincidental.

DEDICATION:

To the readers, you're amazing. Thank you. To my family, we have been through the worst. Now let's get back up and be our best.

And Confidence, may I never lose you again, friend.

CONTENTS

For the Heart sisters, their love has always been dance, but when they settle down to take over the family business, they quickly learn that love is marking them for the realest thing they ever had.
After the worst betrayal, Christmas meets Dru, and for one night, she experiences a love craved and the possibilities of what it could be. She's holding a secret of her own, but will Dru be able to forgive her?

Holiday makes no apologies for keeping men at arm's length. So when Blair dances his way in and demands more, Holiday is ready to throw in the towel quickly. However, that's easier said than done.

Silent Night has no right to be a plus-size dancer in ballroom competitions, yet she is one of the best. All she wants is someone to share the spotlight with, but meeting Dakota makes her wonder is love in the cards to a thick one like her.

This is a NOVELLA!

CHAPTER 1- CHRISTMAS

"Have y'all seen Lex? Silent, have you seen him?" I asked my sister, who had been around this building at least twenty times tonight. Whenever she'd get nervous, she'd run at least a mile. Plus, it was a good warm-up for her. This competition was supposed to be one of the biggest of my dancing career, so naturally, I wanted my man to be here to support me. He was supposed to be here already. I'd texted, called, FaceTimed, and did everything except put the bat signal out for his ass, and still nothing. I had no clue where he was, and I was tired of looking.

Lex and I had been together for the last three years. Up until recently, everything seemed to be going smoothly. There were no big issues. Don't get me wrong, we fight just like every other couple, but it's nothing too serious—not that I thought anyway. But this, not showing up to my competition? He must've lost his damn mind, and that, I just couldn't stand for. But right now, I had to get in the game. I had to be prepared. It wasn't just me competing—my two sisters, Holiday and Silent, were too. As their big sister, I felt it was only right to make sure everything goes perfectly for them. Well, as perfect as it can be.

Looking out into the crowd, I saw my parents. They had pride written all over their faces with smiles a mile long. I grabbed their hands and gave them tight squeezes.

"Y'all ready?" I looked over in both of their directions, waiting on them to answer.

"Shit, I don't know about y'all, but a bitch was born ready!" Holiday yelled, definitely getting the attention of the other dancers. She licked her tongue out at them, and I couldn't do anything but laugh because I already knew how she was when the pressure was on. It was Silent I had to worry about. She always felt like she had to prove to me or others that she was an amazing dancer, but that pressure was coming from herself. I already knew baby sis was cold; she just needed to know it herself.

I let go of Holiday's hand, put my hands on each side of Silent's face, and looked at her.

"Look, we came here to do what we do best. What's that?" I asked, waiting for her to look me in the eyes. She'd had her eyes closed most of the time, calming her nerves. After a few moments of her not answering me, I rubbed my hand over her hair the way our parents used to when they were trying to get her to calm down. My mother and father were award-winning dancers back in their day. They'd been on Soul Train, danced on BET Award shows, and toured with many artists together and separately. Dancing was in our DNA.

After a few deep breaths, Silent looked up at me and responded, "Dance 'til we drop!"

"And that'll never happen. So, are we ready or what?"

Holiday had a personality of her own. She was definitely a wild one, but I loved her, nonetheless. The crowd was cheering our name, and it was time for us to step forward. I looked out into the crowd once again, and my best friend Lisa was coming in, finding her seat. I was about to wave to her when I saw that she looked like she needed to fix herself. Like something wasn't right. She seemed…off. Her hair was all over the place, and her makeup was a bit messed up. Her dress that she'd gotten custom made for the evening was running up her leg. That was odd to me, but Lisa was Lisa's business, not mine.

The music started playing, and as always, our signature move was ready to be executed. I always came out first, then Holiday, and then, of course, Silent. Each of us turning our heads to look at the other, and when I saw the look of confidence on Silent's face, I knew my sisters were ready to tear some shit up.

As the music continued going and we handled our portions of the choreography, I saw Lex. My heart started racing a million miles per minute with joy. I couldn't wait to wrap my arms around him, but something was off about this nigga, too. As I watched him tie his belt back around his pants, I knew I had to have been trippin'. There was no way I saw what I thought I saw. I'm not stupid by any means, and I'ma always put two and two together, but this time, if two and two equaled Lisa and Lex, they asses were as good as grass.

I focused back on the competition at hand, and Silent slid in with her final move, wowing the judges.

"Each of you are light on your feet, just like your mother."

"I love the uniformity and the signatures each girl has made for themselves. I love the sister act."

"Last but not least, each brings their own diversity and presence to the stage."

Holiday, Silent, and I smiled and jumped up and down. No matter how many good things people said about us, we always felt humbled by each judge's opinion, and it wasn't always without criticism. We waited for the judges to give our final scores. As we were standing there waiting, I saw Lex and Lisa staring at one another just a little bit too long. Like they needed to talk about something or like they knew something I didn't, but I was definitely going to find out.

"Ten!"

"Ten!"

"Ten!"

Each judge announced our score, giving us another win under our belt. As happy as I wanted to be, I couldn't even muster up the energy to be happy because all I could think about was Lex and Lisa. I just knew they better not had been doing what I thought they were. Upon us winning, we were given a bonus check of $100,000, trophies, and had a photoshoot to announce our win. Once we were given our earnings, I hugged my sisters, and we went backstage to change our clothes.

"Why you not smilin', bitch? We won!" Holiday jumped up and down and then started twerking in the mirror. I didn't give a damn about any of that...not right now. I put on a fake smile though, just for them so I wouldn't spoil how they were feeling, even though I was dying inside to know the truth.

After a few minutes of us putting on our street clothes, I heard a knock at the door. I went to open it, and it was our parents, Lisa and Lex. My father hugged and kissed each of us, and our mother stood there with tears in her eyes.

"Mommy, why are you making that face?" Tears were threatening to fall. I got up from my chair and wiped the lone tear that she was trying her best to keep from falling on her face.

"I'm just so proud of you girls. You know how to make your father and I proud, and you really did that today, but I already knew you girls were talented, and now, the rest of the world does too."

My mother and father and all of us joined in a hug. Then, I looked over at Lex and Lisa.

"Can y'all give me a moment with my man and my best friend? I wanted to share some news with them."

I had a devilish look on my face, but nobody picked up on it, and I mean, nobody. My parents and sisters left the room. Before they left, I told them to go ahead and go to dinner, and I'd be there to meet them. It was always customary for them to take us out to dinner whenever we had a competition—win or lose.

"Bae, I'm so proud of you—"

I put my hand over his mouth, not wanting to hear the bullshit he was spouting. Lisa looked confused as she walked up to me, smiling.

"Christmas, girl, you already know—"

"Alright, both of y'all shut the fuck up and listen. I don't know if y'all think I'm Booboo the fool or what, and shit, maybe I am since I NEVER thought my best friend would fuck my nigga—"

"Christma—"

"I said shut the fuck up, Lisa! Please, let me finish, and then you can say whatever stupid ass lie I'm sure you gon' tell. Both of y'all really got me fucked up. I mean, Lex, how did you think this was going to go between us? How could you do this?"

Tears then slid down Lisa's face, and I already knew what it was.

"Instead of whoopin' y'all asses like I really want to do, I'ma just let it slide. I really don't even have time for the fuckery either one of y'all tryna put down, and I got better things to worry about than either one of y'all. Lex, I want your shit out of my house tonight, and I don't mean tomorrow, I mean tonight!"

Before walking out of the room, I turned back, looked at Lisa, and shook my head. "And if you didn't know, you dead as fuck to me too!"

Then I exited the room, heartbroken and betrayed, but I knew there had to be something better than this coming my way.

CHAPTER 2- DRUSIEL "THE MUSCLE" GAINS

"Another win for Drusiel "The Muscle" Gains. Dru, how does it feel to still be undefeated? Twenty fights and you haven't lost yet?" a reporter caught my attention as I was leaving the ring. It was true, I hadn't lost a fight, and I didn't plan on it. Most people think boxers are aggressive and crazy, but I'm not. I learned to channel the stresses of life through boxing. I don't wanna hurt nobody for real, but aye, if you get in that ring, you better be prepared to fight for your life with me.

I smiled, noticing the crowd was still going wild. I finally gave my attention to the reporter, who was walking alongside me as I was going back to the locker room.

"Honestly, it's a blessing. My whole career is a blessing, and I'm thankful for everything I've been given. I'm thankful to my trainer, to my family, to my parents—to everyone who helped me along my journey, especially my brother, sister, and best friend. Without my family and friends, and of course, the fans, I wouldn't be shit. Thank you!"

I raised my fists as I left the gym and headed to the locker room. As always, my brother, Blair, and my best friend, Dakota, were waiting for me in the locker room.

"Bruh, I know I say this every time you do it, but damn! I can't even believe how you knocked that nigga out!" Blair gave me a hug, sweat and all. My little brother loved the hell out of me, and I loved him too.

"Aye, small things to a giant, right?" I smirked.

"Small things to a giant? Shut up, nigga. I'm just tryna see when you gon' come back in the gym and show yo' face. You know niggas be surprised we so close. Like we just that different," Dakota admitted. Dakota was my best friend. When his parents died, he came to live with us, so he's really like my brother. When he said he was gonna open up his own gym, I, of course, supported and helped him get business and clientele. My name alone rung many bells, but his story ain't mine—I'll let him tell y'all about that later.

"You right, Kota. So, what's up for tonight? Another win means y'all niggas owe me a night out. What y'all tryna do?"

"Shit, I'm tryna go out and get fucked up. What y'all tryna do?" Blair asked. His young ass knew he couldn't handle his liquor, but I let him make it.

"We can do that. Let me shower, change my clothes, and we'll head out."

I went and hopped in the shower, getting the sweat and blood off me. I could wrap my hands up in the car, something I liked to do just to keep the swelling and shit down. You hit a nigga a couple of times, your hands bound to swell up on some real shit. After my shower, I threw on my clothes and asked where we were headed. Dakota and Blair said they'd seen a couple of bars on their way to the match, so it was only right that we bar hopped.

As soon as we got into the car, we were listening to music, you know, setting the mood. I wasn't really looking for anything but a good time. It had been a while since I'd been out, especially since I'd been training for this fight, but now, I had a little off time, and I wanted to enjoy myself.

We approached a bar; the flashing lights on the outside made it look like a strip joint. Ain't no way I'm payin' to see a bitch get naked when I could get that for free, and my boys knew that. So when they said bar, I knew they had to mean bar.

As soon as we hopped out, I was greeted by the people waiting in line. I had to give a couple of autographs, and of course, I'm always here for the pictures. I never understood people who made their careers off the backs of others but didn't make time to take pictures and sign shit that meant the world to them. Without those people, we wouldn't be shit, so I always made time for them.

After we took a couple of pictures, I was ready to wait in line. I would never be so big that I thought the regular rules that went for other people somehow didn't apply to me. That just wasn't realistic to me, but before I could even get in the line, the bouncer tapped my shoulder and said, "The Muscle? Nigga, you ain't gotta wait in line. You comin' straight through the door. You too humble," the bouncer laughed, and I did too.

I appreciated the special treatment, but I swear it wasn't necessary. I shook up with him and took a picture with him. Again, I love the fans. Me, Blair, and Dakota stepped into the bar, and it turns out that it was more of a club. The music was jumpin', and so was everyone else. The crowd was live, and there were bottle girls walking around with shots and drinks on their carriers.

"Aye baby, let me get one of them," I heard Dakota say. She smiled at the three of us and lowered her tray so we could grab the shots.

"How much I owe you?" I asked. She licked her lips, but I wasn't interested. Something about a woman who worked in a club always threw me off. Y'all can call me judgmental if you want to, but I always felt like they were messing with everyone in the club, and the special attention wasn't really special, if you know what I mean.

"Twenty-five dollars, please."

Money wasn't shit, so I didn't have a problem paying it; I just hoped they would be worth the money.

"To the night!" I shouted, and Blair and Dakota clinked glasses, and threw the shots back. We made our way through the club on some boogie shit. Blair was a dancin' ass nigga, and he always had been, even when we were younger, so I let him get his groove on. Dakota had some girl over in the corner. She was throwing her back up against him, and he had that look in his eyes like he was ready to fuck. I already knew what type of shit he was on, so I had to just let him be himself. I didn't mind groovin' alone. It was all good to me, until something started moving in the corner of my eye. Niggas were always tryin' me because I'm a boxer. They think they can fight and beat me up, so I'm always on high alert. I turned around to see who or what it was coming in my direction. It wasn't a what, but a who, and she wasn't paying me any attention.

Baby was fine as hell. Light-skinned, honey-tipped long dreads, high cheekbones, and a body to die for. She had a little booty, but it fit her body just right, and the way she was smiling while she was dancing turned me on. She had such a pretty smile, and she wasn't in here dressed like half of these other females in here. She had on simple harem jogger pants with a crop top t-shirt and some high-top Chucks. She was all that.

The music changed up a little bit, and I saw her and Blair getting close to one another. I already knew what was about to go down. My brother was a YouTube sensation. Everybody who was into the dance scene already knew him, so when the beat dropped, I knew they were preparing the floor for him. I didn't know who this girl was that was about to try to battle my brother, but I knew she was about to get shit jumpin'. I could tell by the way they were dancing. I was surprised, because the way she looked, and the way she moved, I felt like she was on some classical dance type stuff, but she was givin' my brother the business with the way she moved her hips, and her arms were winding around her body like a clock. She was all that.

The crowd was hype, and I was cheering my brother on. By the time the music stopped, they were both out of breath and smiling. My brother gave her a hug, and I wondered if he knew her. I made my way closer to the two of them and interrupted their conversation.

"Ok, bruh, I see you ain't come to play."

Blair had sweat drippin' off of him, but he laughed, "Hell yeah. I been waitin' on the opportunity to battle this girl. This is Christmas. She just won a dance competition tonight."

Christmas looked up at me and smiled. I returned her smile. "Hi, I'm Drusiel Gains. It's nice to meet you, Christmas."

"Likewise."

Blair looked at us, and he already knew what was up. "Look, bruh, I'ma let y'all get up. I'ma head over here and chill with Kota for a minute."

I nodded my head and gave my little brother a hug. Christmas and I stood still for a moment, just staring at each other. She then laughed.

"What's so funny?" I asked, wondering why she was giggling

when neither one of us had said anything.

"I'm sorry, I'm a little drunk, and I'm tryna laugh to keep from crying for real."

"Crying? What a beautiful girl like you got to be cryin' about? You took home a W today from what I hear. Winners don't cry, baby."

She laughed again, but then her smile quickly disappeared when she looked toward the door. I turned around to see what she was staring at, and a dude had walked in with another girl. From the look on Christmas' face, I could tell she knew them.

"You good?" I grabbed her arm, and she looked up at me. I ain't no punk ass dude, but touching her, something came over me.

"I would be better if I weren't here. I came here to get away from them." She nodded her head in their direction.

"Ex boyfriend with a new girlfriend?"

"Something like that. Try was just my boyfriend a few hours ago and my best friend."

That was some foul ass shit. Even though I hadn't experienced anything like that, I could only imagine how she was feeling.

"So, you gon' leave because of this nigga? They wanna make you uncomfortable, don't let them win. Don't let them steal your win."

"You don't even know me, why you willin' to be all nice to me?"

I could tell she was clearly guarded due to the situation at hand, but I was a good dude, and I had every intention on showing her that. "Because you're a woman, and no woman should be treated like that. Just follow my lead."

I could tell she was hesitant, but when I stuck my hand out, she took it with a smile. I led her back out onto the dance floor, and we started dancing. The record changed to something slow and smooth. I grabbed her close to me, wrapping my arms around her waist. Her perfume was so strong, but in a good way. I could tell it wasn't that cheap shit—she looked like the type of woman to wear Chanel.

Her face brushed up against mine, and I distanced myself to

spin her around so dude could see that she was being treated well in his absence. She giggled when her chest brushed back up against mine.

"How'd you learn to dance like this?" she inquired.

"You don't have a brother who knows how to dance and don't somehow learn a thing or two. I used to go with him to his dance classes and shit, and one of them was in traditional dancing. Plus, my sister is getting married next year, so she got us all on high alert."

"That's actually smart. Most men wouldn't want to do something like that."

"I ain't most men, Christmas. Speaking of which, your parents really named you Christmas? Like, that's not a dancing name?"

"Ha! No, my parents loved the holidays, so there's me, my sister Silent and Holiday. My parents were on one."

"Nah, they was on some different shit, and I can dig it."

As we were dancing and conversing, I could feel some eyes on me, like somebody was staring a hole into the back of my head. I turned around, looked to the right of us, and her ex was staring at us, watching enviously. I would be too. Christmas was fine as hell.

"Damn, dude really pressed behind you," I whispered into Christmas' ear. She looked over and saw him, but I could feel she was relaxed under my touch.

"You snooze, you lose, huh?" she said back, and I laughed.

We continued dancing until the song changed, and then she said she needed to use the restroom. I had been in clubs like this when shit went down with females, and people wantin' to grab them in the bathroom or disturb their entrance and shit, so I couldn't let her go by herself.

"Here, let me escort you that way."

I grabbed her hand and led her through the crowd, making sure she got there safely. I checked the inside to make sure everything was on the up and up. Then I came back out and stood guard of the door to make sure she was good. When she came out, she was laughing.

"What's going on now? Another cry to keep from laughing

situation?"

"Nah, of course not. I'm just surprised how sweet you are. A protective boxer? Unheard of."

"Is it, and oh, you know who I am, huh?"

"Doesn't everybody?"

I shrugged my shoulders, and then I noticed she was swaying. Christmas was drunk as hell, and I wanted to make sure she was going to be ok.

"How you gettin' home? You drive?"

"I did. I got my keys; I'll be ok."

"Nah, ain't no way. How 'bout this. I had one drink. We can go get something to eat and then I'll make sure you get home. I'm not on no stalker type shit, but I wanna make sure you get home okay and safe. How that sound?"

She made a face, and I knew she wasn't comfortable, but there was no other option for her. I wasn't about to let something bad happen to her.

"What about your brother? Didn't you drive?" she asked, still swaying.

"I never drive to a match. Driving takes me out the mood, and I need to focus before it happens, so I rode with my trainer, and then my brother drove. He a grown ass man, he can take care of himself. Plus, he's here with my best friend, Dakota. He'll be alright."

"Well...what did you have in mind for food? I could eat, and I know it'll help me sober up."

I nodded my head and grabbed her hand. I threw my hand up in the direction of Dakota and Blair and walked outside with Christmas. She pointed to her car, and I told her to wait on the sidewalk so I could go and get it. She had a nice little Mercedes, midnight blue with the chrome handles. I guess this dancing shit must've been lucrative for her. I turned on the car, scooting the seat back some to get my legs going and then pulled up. I got out of the car and went to open her door.

"A gentleman, too? That's really nice."

"This your shit, of course I'ma open the door for you, and

again, you're a woman. You got it."

I grabbed her hand and helped her get in because she was so drunk. When we got in the car, Christmas' phone automatically connected, and jazz music started playing. I could vibe with it. It was two o'clock in the morning, and the only thing open was Waffle House. I pulled into the parking lot, and she had a smirk on her face.

"This is a good move!"

"The best move, baby."

I parked the car right in front of the building, and then rushed to the other side to get her out of the car.

"You sure you should be eating this? I don't want you to purge after you eat all this grease."

"I can eat this shit and pay for it tomorrow. I'm sure I'll find a way to get the extra calories off." I winked at her. I didn't mean it sexually, but seductively it came out anyway.

"Boy, come on and let's get some food."

I grabbed her hand and then opened the door with the other. We took a seat at the bar and ordered our food. Everybody knows what goes on in Waffle House. It's the place to be.

We sat there talking, getting to know one another as best as we could with the little time we did have. When the food came, we were still in the middle of our conversation, and it seemed like Christmas was on her way to finding herself sober. She wasn't swaying, and her eyes didn't look as glossed over.

After we were done, I pulled out my wallet. I saw Christmas reaching for hers, and I put my hand in front of hers. "Don't do that, baby. I got this."

"I can pay for my own meal, Dru."

"Yeah, you can, but you shouldn't have to. When you're in my presence, you won't."

Christmas wrapped her arm around me and tilted her head on my shoulder. Having her against me felt so good. I hadn't been in the presence of a woman I actually liked in a long time. I wasn't tryna rush and get married, but being around her was nice. After I paid and left a tip, we walked away and got into her car. She gave me directions to her house, and I told her when I got there, I'd catch a Lyft back so she didn't have to worry about dropping me back off.

We arrived in front of her home in twenty-five minutes. I was lowkey dreading leaving her because I didn't know if I'd ever see her again and I wasn't going to ask for her number. If she wanted me to have it, she'd give it to me.

I turned off her car and went around to the side to let her out once again.

"Thank you for the night. You don't know how you saved my night for me. I don't know what's going to happen when I go in the house, but for tonight, I feel good."

"That's all I wanted," I said, as I brushed her dreads from her face, pulling them behind her ear to get a better look at her face. She was as beautiful as she was when I'd first seen her. I'm not a sensitive nigga, but the moonlight hittin' her face was just right.

She grabbed my hands and looked up at me for a second, and I smiled. She then started to walk away, so I pulled my phone out of my pocket. I hadn't checked it the whole time I was with her, and I didn't have a need to, not when I was with Christmas. She kept my mind occupied with her conversation and her beautiful face. I really liked how she opened up to me about her nigga, well, ex-nigga Lex and her backstabbing ass best friend, Lisa. I could tell she was feeling me as much as I was feeling her, and I hoped one day, we would reconnect some type of way.

I was pulling up the Lyft app when I heard her drop her keys on the porch. I turned around, and she was throwing up all over her front porch. I slid my phone back into my pocket, laughing, grabbed her keys from the ground and opened her door.

"Don't look at me, Dru. Just...just loo-"

I turned back around, and she was throwing up again, this time, on herself.

"Damn, baby. You got it that bad, huh?"

Tears were coming out of her eyes. I could tell she was embarrassed, but there was no need for that. Shit happens, even and especially when you don't want it to. Once the door was open, I picked her up. I ain't give a shit about no throw-up. I get blood on myself all the time—throw-up is just another bodily fluid. I carried her into the house and looked around. She was almost passed out in my arms. From the hallway, I could see a light that was turned on, so I followed it and carried her to her room. There was a bathroom inside, and she took straight off into it.

I sat down on the footstool she had in her room and called out to her. "Christmas, you okay?

"Just…give…me…a…second!" she shouted back. I could hear her tossing up everything in her stomach.

A few minutes later, I heard the shower turn on, and I knew that was my cue to go. I got up and was going to sneak out, but then she stuck her head out the door.

"Do you mind staying? I know I don't know you, but I really don't want to be alone. From the looks of it in the closet, Lex did at least come and get his shit, so I'll be here all night. Will you just stay long enough for me to fall asleep?"

In a short amount of time, I had grown fond of her. I didn't want the night to end anyway, so I agreed.

"Yeah, go ahead and handle your business. I'll go wait in the living room for you."

The door closed back and I made my way back into the living room. I could tell this house was all her. From the ceilings to the floor, I could tell she'd decorated this whole place. I wouldn't have even known she had a man had it not had the stench of a nigga or a few of his items left inside the house. I scoped out the kitchen and then the dining room. I even looked at the pictures she had of her family on the wall. There were so many pictures of her and her sisters, I could tell she was close to them the same way I was close to Blair and Dakota.

After a few minutes, she came back out with her robe and bunny slippers on. Shit was cute as fuck. Her dreads were tied up in a bun, and she was smiling.

"Feeling better?"

"Like a brand new baby. Sometimes, you just gotta get that shit out, you know?"

"Oh, I know exactly what you mean."

She came around the couch and took a seat. "You wanna find something to watch on Amazon Prime?"

"Yeah, we can do that."

She cut the TV on, and the first thing on was a recap of my match. "We ain't gotta watch that."

"Sure we do! I missed the match. I haven't missed one in a while."

"So, you a fan?" I smirked, turning around to look at her.

"I didn't say all that, but I'm up on the shit. Now hush, let me see what you was doin' tonight."

We sat back on the couch and watched. I normally hated seeing myself in a recap, but with Christmas, it was cool. "That's probably why you're a good dancer, you have good footwork."

"Check you out, paying attention."

She laughed and hit my shoulder. I grabbed her and started tickling her. It felt so natural with her, I couldn't help it. I pinned her down on the couch, and her legs were kicking. Her laugh was so infectious, it made me laugh too. She was turning her head, and her dreads got loose. They fell over her face, and I loved looking at it, so I moved them out the way. In that moment, she just looked so angelic, so perfect, that I couldn't help but kiss her.

Her lips were so juicy and wet. As soon as I kissed them, it was like having a drink of water. I was thirsty for her. Her arms reached around my neck, and my body fell into hers perfectly. I grabbed the sides of her long legs and wrapped them around me. She pulled me in as close as she could. I could smell her body wash, and it meshed well with her natural body scent.

I pulled away from her feeling the moment getting too heated. She'd just got out of a relationship, and I didn't want to be some type of rebound sex, but when I stopped, she gave me this innocent look, like she didn't want me to. I knew then that I was about to take baby down. I leaned back on top of her and started kissing her again. I'm a fighter but an affectionate nigga too. Her fingernails were scaling my back, lightly scratching me, and that shit had me turned on.

We both were breathing like dogs in heat, and I couldn't stand her breasts poking my chest through her robe. I had to see what she was working with. Slowly, I untied her robe and let it fall off of her. She was butt ass naked underneath, and her body was just as nice as I knew it would be.

I trailed kisses down her cheeks, to her neck, and then my mouth found her nipples. Her breath sped up, and I sucked her titties like my life depended on it. I used my left hand to squeeze the other as her body started grinding up against me. She wanted the dick, and I wanted to give it to her.

"Take me into my bedroom. Pick me up like you did to carry me in the house," she whispered.

"You liked that shit?"

"I loved it."

I licked her bottom lip and sucked on it, and then carried her to the back for a night neither of us would ever forget…

CHAPTER 3- HOLIDAY

Two years later

"Throw that ass in a circle! Throw that ass in a circle!" I sang as I rounded my hips in the mirror. It was my birthday, and all I wanted to do was celebrate and turn up. It had been a long time since I'd actually been out. Tonight, I just wanted to have a good time without having to worry about or think about anybody but myself. I just wanted to dance for the hell of it, and that was gon' be that on that.

Thankfully, Christmas came over the day before and gave me a fresh retwist. I couldn't help it, when she started her dreads, I had to start mine too because they looked so good! I was in the mirror getting ready for the night. I had so many plans, but it just didn't seem like enough time. I had dinner plans with my family, like I did every year. My parents and my sisters always made sure I ate good for my birthday, and we were supposed to be going out for crab legs. Thank the lord! Amen! After that, Christmas, Silent, and I would be going out to the club to dance the night away. People thought because we danced professionally, we didn't enjoy dancing outside of our jobs. The fuck y'all think we dance for, shits and giggles? I still loved a good street battle, and tonight, I was going to get just that, if I was lucky.

I finished up my makeup, making sure my eyebrows and eyelashes were dramatic, because shit, I am, and then slipped into a V-cut, gold sequined dress that stopped right above my thigh. I finished my look with a Pandora bracelet that my parents had been getting me charms for the last two or three years. I had a soft pink and gold watch on the other wrist, and several rings adorned my fingers. I'd planned to wear my gold stilettos with the pointy heel, but all this was just for my parents. Inside my bag was where the real magic was. In my bag, I had my black activewear leggings, a tank top, and my yellow crop top to go on top. Now, anytime I pulled out this specific outfit, everybody knew shit was about to get real different. They already knew I was about to throw down and have a good time, and since it was my birthday, I was more than entitled to the good time that was about to occur.

I hadn't wanted to mention it, and I still don't, but just to catch y'all up, last year, year twenty-three was terrible for me. I thought being in a committed relationship was awful, but not being in one is even worse. I dated this guy briefly, and I thought we were on the same page, but we clearly weren't. I thought we were on some chill shit; some hang out type shit. I didn't realize that when I said we could see other people, that WE COULDN'T SEE OTHER PEOPLE! I had it that way for a reason. I've done the committed thing a million times over, and I literally mean, a million. I've always been the one who is trying to keep shit together, but then the niggas I date, they either don't want to only be with me or being with me is too much. Bet. So I thought I'd make it easy for the last dude and say we could keep it casual.

That worked a solid month before he started following me places, popping up all the time, and getting mad when I'd be with other guys. And don't let me take a picture and post it with a nice outfit on. I was getting cussed out, called all types of names and all types of crazy shit. I figured then I just was meant to be by myself forever, maybe. There was only one person I'd ever consider maybe settling down for at this point, but what's meant to be will be. No matter how hard you try to fight fate.

I didn't even realize I was caught up in my thoughts until I heard my phone ringing. I looked to the side, and it was my dad. A smile caressed my face when I saw "Daddy" pop up on my phone. I loved my parents. One thing I could say about them was they'd always been there for us, and they were amazing parents. They took care of us, encouraged us, and they loved us, and for that, I'd forever be grateful.

"Hi, Daddy!"

"Hi, baby girl. We're headed to the restaurant now."

"No, tell the truth. We're pulling up at the restaurant. We just wanted to give you some extra time since you're always late!"

I heard my mother scold with a laugh. It was true. I was always the one who was late, and I definitely wasn't good at planning shit. This was exactly why my parents and sisters normally just asked me what I wanted to do, and they made it happen for me.

"Ok, ok. No need to point out the obvious, but I'm actually done. I just need to get my keys and head on out."

"Well then do it, because I'm starving. By the way, happy birthday, baby!" my mom yelled, and then the phone hung up. I had a smile a mile wide on my face because I couldn't wait to get together with my family one more time. I checked my makeup one more time to make sure that it was on point. My hair was perfectly laying over my shoulders, and I looked so good. I grabbed my keys and the clutch that matched my dress. I looked perfect for the night I had ahead. Before I left the house, I made sure to grab my bag so that I didn't ultimately ruin the night I had made for myself.

Thirty minutes later, I was at the restaurant, ready to eat! I thought about it and realized we dead ass just dressed up to eat some crab legs, knowing good and damn well we were going to get messy. Ask me if I care though? One thing is for certain, and two things for sure, I was bustin' them crab legs no matter if I was butt naked or not. After I parked my car, I got out and headed toward my sisters.

"Happy birthday, Holiday! You ready for tonight?" Christmas leaned in and asked me. She was whispering on purpose. Our parents paid a lot of money for us to dance properly. Street dancing… well, I'm not going to say they hated it, but it was frowned upon. They felt we should be using our talents to be paid and to compete. I liked to compete, just not always for national broadcasts.

I nodded my head and then pulled Silent in for a hug as well. She smiled and kissed me on the cheek. She already knew what was up for the night, and we were all in the mood to have a good time, it seemed.

Once we were all together, I, of course, hugged my parents, and then the hostess led us to a table that was long enough for us all to sit at. I ordered the king crab, like I always did, and then waited for the food to come out. We sat, talked, and laughed. Then I felt my phone vibrate from my purse. I looked at it and smiled.

B: *I wish I could be with you tonight, but I know how that goes.*

I licked my lips just thinking about him. There was no way I was bringing anyone around my family, especially when we weren't together. I hadn't been seeing anyone else, but he didn't need to know that. Things were going well between us so far, but that's how they always were. Perfect for a little while, and then they'd blow up, and that's what I was trying to avoid.

"Holiday, do you hear me?" my father asked me. I looked up at him with a smile.

"I'm sorry, Daddy. I didn't even hear you. What did you say?"

"I asked what your plans were after dinner? You and your sisters going out to have a good time?"

I looked at them, trying to conceal our plans for the evening, but that was hard to do.

"I don't really have anything mapped out. We might go and get some food and stuff, you know."

"You just ain't never been able to lie, girl, so don't start now. Listen, since it's your birthday, I'm not gonna come down on you, but what I do want to know is how everything with the studio is coming?" my mom asked, looking over at me, Silent, and Christmas. The truth was, we were three of the best dancers in the city, but we were also hard to work with because of all of our training, our comfortability, and we knew more than a lot of the other studios and dancers out there. The studio was still doing well, and we were booked to the max, but it wouldn't have hurt to diversify our clientele a bit.

"Everything is good, Mom. How are you and Dad? Y'all enjoying retirement?"

My dad looked at my mom and grabbed her hand. One of these days, I hoped I'd have what they did, but my parents were a different breed of people. One I wasn't sure I'd be able to find to match what I needed. I was the goofy one. I laugh a lot, smile a lot, dance a lot, eat a lot. I do absolutely everything in excess. I was a dramatic person and needed someone who could go along with that, but I hadn't had too much luck completely finding what I needed yet. Until then, I'd be with myself, like I said before.

Dinner moved along great, and I busted those crab legs out the frame. They were delicious. As always, my parents got me another charm to go on my bracelet. My mom said she loved to watch the charms jingle around my wrist whenever I danced, and my father gave me money. Christmas got me a gift card to Midas so I could get new tires. It wasn't that I didn't have the money to do it, I was just too lazy to drop my car off or sit up there and let them put on a brand new set. Silent reached under the table and pulled out a bag. It was medium-sized and red, my favorite color. I smiled, pulled it to myself, and opened it up. Inside was a Jaclyn Hill Morphe palette that I hadn't been able to find anywhere, a new set of makeup brushes, and an appointment card for one of the up and coming lash-ticians in the city.

I was very happy with my gifts. I got up from the table, walked around, and gave everybody a hug. I couldn't have been happier to have this moment, but now, it was time for some fun. My dad paid for the food, and I hugged and kissed them one last time before my sisters, and I walked outside, headed towards our cars.

"Y'all bring your bags? We ain't got no time to be stopping."

"Yes, Holiday. I should be asking you that, Ms. I Don't Know How to Plan Anything," Christmas retorted.

"Alright, you think you funny, but you ain't, now hush. I'ma meet y'all there?"

Christmas and Silent nodded, and I got into my car. On the way over to "The Attic," the place most people went to see the rawest and coldest form of dancing, I wondered how the night was going to go, and if it would be as hype as I thought it was. I saw the flyers going around, and I was always down for a good time, so I'd be devastated if we got to this party, and nothing was jumpin'. On the ride over, at the red lights, I changed my clothes, the same way I knew my sisters did. The only thing left was for me to put on my shoes, which after I parked my car, I did just that. I'd been driving barefoot since I slid on my pants at a red light.

Getting out of the car, I saw Christmas and Silent were dressed, looking not so different from me. Shit had me dying laughing. They already knew what I was going to wear, because this was my thing—crop tops and tanks. I thought it was sweet they dressed like me.

"Ok, so it's not bad enough we get made fun of for our names, but we got y'all two out here dressed like we the Brady Bunch or the OMG Girls? That's cute!" I laughed, and Christmas hit me in the arm.

"Shut up and come on. It's your birthday, so I wanted you to feel special. Like we were tryna do a lil' sumn' sumn' for you, you know?"

I wrapped my arms around my sisters and smiled, as we walked into the building. As soon as we got inside, people were standing around us, laughing, smiling, and high-fiving us. I couldn't have been happier to have such a good dance reputation with a lot of the other dancers here. My sisters and I had battled a lot of them, but we had mad respect for them, just like they did us.

The announcer was walking up to the stage, preparing everyone for the crews and the people who would be dancing when I got a text on my phone. I took it out of my pocket and saw B had sent me another text.

B: So, you thought you was gon' come to The Attic and not speak to me? You bein' bogus asf, but you look good as hell. I love you, beautiful. Happy birthday.

My whole heart felt like it was about to jump out of my chest. I looked around to see if I could find him, but I had no such luck. Everywhere I looked, it was empty, but I had a smile plastered across my face so big, that no matter where he was, he would see it. I couldn't even think of what to say to write back. In my heart, I knew it was possible that I loved him too, but I was too afraid to say that. I didn't know if we should take it to the next step because he used to be a hoe, and once a hoe, always a hoe. People rarely change, but what do I know?

We got up on stage after they announced us as "The Spirit Sisters" since we get everyone in the mood for the "Holidays." We loved battling crews, because we were our own force. When we were together, wasn't shit stoppin', and everything was poppin'!

Needless to say, this night was going to be one for the books. This would be our last chance to dance for fun for a little while. We had a wedding coming up, and several daytime talk shows to attend, so we had to live it up one last time.

Three Months Later

"Silent, we have a few things on the schedule today. One being dance practice for the show competition and that Jones' wedding party that's coming in at three. Juda and Lou called out, but I called in your sisters. They're in room three with the men your parents arranged for the competition. Holiday said she gotcha and Christmas said you irky as fuck, but she'll be here and you owe her." Rena, my assistant, said.

"What studio they from?"

"Dream maker's studio." Soon as she said that, I rolled my eyes. They swear they produced the best dancers and they weren't. Up until a year ago, we all had partners we danced with for years until we all decided to take over the family business.

Before I continue, let me introduce myself. The name's Silent Night Heart, and before you say it, I already know. My parents met during Christmas at a professional competition over thirty years ago in Argentina. They were going against each other but when they saw one another at first glance, they knew they were destined or at least that's what they say. I guess it was true because a year after dating, they got married on that same day because it was their favorite holiday of the year. That's how my sisters and I got the names we did. Leaving their partners behind, they started their own ballroom studio and dance club and taught us everything we know. Of course, we could do all the dances, but we all had our skills that made us world-renowned dancers. Christmas was the oldest and the more in tune with herself. She likes to say nobody could touch her when it came to the Jive, Argentine Tango, or the Quick Step. She picked up the dances so quickly that master seemed like the name we should have gave for her. Holiday was the middle child and the free spirit of us all. She mastered East Coast Swing, Rumba, and the Bachata. Then was me, the thick girl who shouldn't dance yet could get it with the best of them. That's probably why everyone called me Meanie so much it started to stick. When it can to Salsa, Samba, or the Pasadoble, I was your girl and I knew it too.

"Fine. Let me rehearse and come get us twenty minutes before the Jones party so we can shower, and make sure my parents are flying in a week before," I said before entering in room two.

We had been practicing nonstop for the past three hours and the irritation was written all over my face. I don't know what our parents were thinking hiring these guys. There was no connection between my partner and I. I didn't trust him to do lifts. As great as the choreography is, it just isn't going to work. One rule me and my sisters had was no dating anyone in the industry. Our parents hated that because they felt we would meet our soulmate the same way they met. Wrong. My ex, King, was my partner for two years, and as great as a friend that he is, the connection wasn't there. At twenty-two, I wanted a man who could make me feel like dancing did.

"You need to lead me, not the other way around."

"Silent, I'm trying."

"1,2,3,4,5,6,7,8. 1,2,3,4,5,6,7,8. Christmas, pick up your movements! Silent, connect with him! Right now, you look awkward! The rumba is supposed to be sexy!" my sister, Holiday, yelled, drilling us over and over again. She had it easy; her partner, Jonas, was cute, funny, and knew how to move.

Meanwhile, Christmas' partner couldn't do lifts, and mine was so weak that it showed in our dancing. I constantly found myself leading because he refused to do so. How the hell is he a competitive dancer? I don't know. I don't know what my parents were thinking, but these matches clearly weren't going to work. The Rumba is a dance with fast and slow movements to Afro-Cuban music. Every year people would buy tickets to our Christmas celebration and this year was no exception. We sold out in hours for the first two weeks and our VIP Christmas Eve show sold out in two hours. Those tickets alone sold for three thousand apiece.

"You think after this we can go out and chill?"

"I don't date people in the industry," I replied quickly. This boy couldn't even take the lead in a dance, so I know damn well he couldn't go on a date and deal with me. I had a slick mouth; we all did, and we could back that shit up.

"Less talking, more dancing. 1,2,3 lift," Day scolded us like she did anytime she choreographed a dance.

"Donnie, I weigh one twenty soaking wet. If you drop me one more time, I'm fucking you up," Christmas said through gritted teeth.

"I'm trying. You're heavier than I expected," he said.

"Look, Holiday, I quit. Jonas cool or whatever, but Silent and I are struggling with these guys. His weak ass can't bench press one fucking twenty. We need partners with upper body strength."

"It's not that bad."

"Lift me," Christmas demanded, only to be dropped.

"She's right, Day. Jonas is good, but we need better partners. And we need them quick because we have less than a month to rehearse before the shows start. Don't let your attraction get in the way of the show."

"You right. My bad, y'all. We can get Brent to do open auditions over the weekend. I'm about to call mom and dad and tell them that their choices aren't a good fit," Holiday said, caving in. If she wanted to fuck with ole boy on her own time, cool, but since the contract said they were a package deal, there was no way we could use just him.

"Excuse me, girls. You need to get ready for the wedding party," Rena said. Leaving my sisters, I went into my office to shower. Each of us had our own office with a built-in shower, a walk-in closet, and a bed that came out the wall with the hit of a button in case we were too tired to drive. Turning the shower on, I stripped out my sweaty clothes and washed my hair, thinking about what I wanted Santa to bring me. Truthfully, forget the money, cars, and clothes, send me a thug with a python for a dick anytime. Since I wanted to be comfortable, I settled on some black Spanxs and a black half shirt because Kim had said her family was going to need a lot of work. After checking my emails and eating a salad to tide me over 'til later, I went to kick it with my sisters 'til our appointment showed up.

"Y'all ready to warm up? I choreographed a nice Samba-Hip Hop routine. Kim suggested something sexy and fun."

CHAPTER 5- DAKOTA

"I'm not gonna argue with you, 'Kota! You're like a brother to me, too, so you need to get your ass over to this dance studio before I flip the hell out on you. Don't ruin my fucking day, please! GET HERE NEEEOOW!"

I had to move the phone away from my ear to stop from hearing Kim's mouth. She wanted me to do this stupid ass dance sequence in her wedding, and the whole time, all I could think about was how Blair and Dru were better suited for this shit. I couldn't lie, no matter how close all of us had been, and no matter how much time passed, I sometimes still felt out of place. When I lost my parents, even though I went to live with Dru, Blair, and Kim, and their parents became my parents who really loved and raised me, it's nothing like having the people you were supposed to have in this world, for real.

Kim had already hung up the phone before I could say anything else. She already knew I was going to come, but I was running late tryna finish lifting weights and shit. Sometimes, that was the only thing that would really help relax me. My mind had been racing the last couple of months. I ain't gettin' no younger, and I'm ready to settle down. All this sleeping with this woman and sleeping with this woman was getting old. It was old even before now. All I really want is to come home to one woman and settle the fuck down, but that shit hard as fuck to do.

I knew what I wanted and always had. I wanted a smart and driven woman. Somebody I could call my own and don't have to share, somebody I can give the world to and they give it back to me, but these young thots, they for everybody. All I want is a woman, not a hoe!

I raised up off the bench where I was lifting weights and put them back down beside me. Looking over into the mirror, I could see I was sweating, so I knew I needed to shower real quick and then head over to the studio. I didn't want to do this dancing shit, but if that's what Kim wanted, then that's what would get done. I just wanted her to be happy, even if it made me uncomfortable as fuck. It wasn't that I couldn't do a lil' two-step, I just didn't want to have to do a whole choreographed dance. I thought that was stupid as fuck, but it ain't my wedding, and it's not my life. It ain't gon' kill me.

Luckily, there were showers at my gym, so I didn't have to go anywhere. Like I said, I had planned on going, but I was running behind. I hopped in the shower real quick and dried off. I was already running about thirty minutes behind, and I hoped they weren't waiting for me to get it together for them to practice. Then I would actually feel bad. I grabbed a pair of jeans and a t-shirt. I already knew this was about to be an even bigger mess because I was supposed to be wearing what we'd wear at the reception for the dance, a lil' dress rehearsal type of thing to make sure everybody was comfortable, but if they were comfortable, I'd have to just be too.

I grabbed my keys and made sure I had my wallet and headed to the car. A nigga was already late, so I wasn't about to be racing through traffic. I might as well take my time and get there safe, but there wasn't really any traffic. It was the stoplights that kept getting me for real. Finally, after six or so stoplights and more lefts than anybody should have to take, I had arrived at the dance studio.

"Man, I'm too big of a nigga to be doin' this shit," I said as I shook my head. I ain't fat by no means, but I'm tall as hell, like six-foot-six or seven and a thick ass body because all I do is workout. My whole body is inked the fuck out, and for real, I'm too gangsta of a nigga to be movin' my body the way they wanted me to. But again, for Kim, I would do anything.

I shut the car door and headed inside. I could hear Kim's loud ass mouth all the way from the front of the building. There was a woman at the front desk, and I figured I should check in with her first. I walked over to the front, and she smiled, licking her lips, but I wasn't interested at all.

"Hey, I'm looking for—" I didn't even get to get my sentence out before I heard Kim's mouth again.

"Oh, now you show up. I swear to God, Dakota, if you wasn't family, I'd kick yo' ass!"

"Nah, you mean if I wasn't this big, you'd try to. What's good?"

Kim's eyes softened and she ran into my arms. As always, I picked her up and gave her a tight hug. Kim really embraced me like I was Dru or Blair, and the love between us was mutual.

"What's good is you need to come back here with me. I've got him!" Kim said over her shoulder to the lady at the desk as she pulled me closer to the back.

When we got back there, Kim introduced me to Christmas, but she looked familiar. I couldn't figure out from where though. She seemed like someone I'd met before. Then she introduced me to Holiday, who I found out was Christmas' sister. They parents must've been trippin' on acid naming them that. Now, I ain't no soft nigga, but it seemed like the whole world stopped when I heard footsteps coming up from behind me.

"This is Silent, right?" Kim asked.

She shook her head up and down. "Silent Night, but Silent is perfect. Is this who we were waiting on?" She looked up at me and smiled. I can't lie. I had to clear my throat because it felt dry. Christmas and Holiday were pretty, but Silent? Nah, she was everything. She was thick in all the right places, her voice was smooth like water going down your throat, and even with sweat drippin' down her face and body, she just looked amazing.

"Yes, this is Dakota. Dru and Blair are in the other room. They haven't come out here yet. Thank you so much for waiting for my other brother to get here. He's annoying but promises to cooperate," Kim giggled, and I damn sure was going to cooperate with whatever Ms. Silent had to say. Damn, she was really beautiful.

When Blair and Dru came out of the other room, I walked over to them and shook them up, giving them both hugs.

"What up, 'Kota? Fuck you was doin'?" Dru thought he was finna interrogate me. Dude thought because he was a boxer, I couldn't handle him. That was my fault though. I made that nigga that cocky.

"Dude, shut yo' ass up, but what I'm tryna figure out is if y'all saw the three sisters? They all pretty, but Silent and Holiday—"

"Aye, you don't even know them like that. Silent seem more like yo' speed anyway," Blair rushed and said. I turned my face up at him.

"Fuck wrong with you? I mean, you right, but Holiday—"

"So, you gon' just disregard what I said? Silent is the one for you, man." Blair hit me on my chest twice and started walking away.

Dru was standing there like he'd seen a ghost. Normally, he'd get in on the clowning and acting a fool, but he wasn't doing that, and I knew something wasn't right.

"What's wrong, bro? You okay?"

"Man...I've never been better. I'ma get up with you after this is over, aite?"

I didn't know what to say to that, but I watched him as he walked in the direction of Christmas, who had been bent over stretching. When she looked up, she looked like she was about to throw up all over herself. I didn't know what was going on, but that shit wasn't my business. My focus was all on Silent—that was who I wanted to talk to.

"Alright, so everybody is going to get a partner. It looks like Blair and Holiday, since they match up in height, and they complement each other well. Christmas and Dru, since they've been over there talking to one another, and that leaves 'Kota and Silent. Everybody okay with that?" Kim inquired, and nobody had a complaint, especially not me. Shit again, whatever Silent said, I was going to do it.

She walked over to me with a smile. "You sure you ready for this?"

"Hell nah, I don't even know what we about to do for real."

"Well, just follow me. I won't lead you wrong."

"I believe that, but as a man, isn't it my job to lead?"

She made a face and then a giggle slipped out. "Normally, I would say yes, but as a woman and as the person who knows the choreography, let me show you how to lead, and then I'll turn it over to you. How's that sound?"

"Perfect, baby. I mean, Silent."

She nodded her head, and then the music began playing. Kim's partner was, of course, her fiancé Ted, AKA Teddy the Man. We had been calling him that since high school. Kim met dude when she was with someone else, and she kept sleeping on him. She thought he was soft and that she was out of his league, but when the guy she was seeing got loud and was tryna get a little crazy with Kim, it was Ted who beat the hell out of him. They expelled him from school because of how badly he beat him up, and since then, we've been calling him that.

Silent, Christmas, and Holiday took to the front of us, each showing us the routine we'd need to learn and get down in just a matter of days, but I couldn't focus on anything but Silent.

"It seems like you're either not getting it, or you want to be here longer. Which one is it? I'm a perfectionist, and I need you to be on point!" She slapped her hands together. She was so short, but it was hilarious to me the way she commanded attention with everything she said and the way her body moved.

"I think it's a little bit of both. Is that a crime that I want to hold a beautiful woman in my arms just a little while longer?"

She took a step back and looked up at me. "Listen, I don't like to mix business with pleasure—"

"So, I'm not your type?" I stepped closer to her, bridging the gap between us.

"I didn't say you wasn't my type. What I said was—"

"Was that you don't mix business with pleasure. Well, check this out, I'm not leaving here today until I get your phone number. I won't call or text or none of that until this whole wedding stuff is over. What you think about that?" Yeah, I was puttin' the moves on her, but it was something about Silent, other than her name, that was different, and I could tell.

Maybe it was the way she walked or the way she danced, but I had to know something about her. Just watching her move along to the music, I could tell she was a passionate dancer and really took her career seriously. Maybe she didn't wanna mix business with pleasure because she wouldn't be able to control one of them. I didn't give a damn—I just needed to be able to get with her after all of this.

"How about this, you show me you can learn the steps, and I'll give you my number?"

"When?"

"Go home and practice what we did today, and if you've improved when you come in tomorrow, my number is yours."

I smirked, and she started walking away, but then she turned back around just slightly and looked over her shoulder, "And you can use the number before all of this is over."

"Bet!" I guess all that business with pleasure shit was bogus. It had been a long time since I went home in a good mood, but today, that shit just changed.

CHAPTER 6- CHRISTMAS

I'm not gonna even try and lie; the second I saw Dru, my stomach dropped into my asshole. I was feeling so good and so confident until I saw him. I came up with the routine, and of course, we learned it in no time. Compliments of good dance training. It was nothing for us to come up with something and learn the routine. I was really proud of Silent for the way she was hitting the moves precisely and executed teaching them just as well. I low key had been wanting her to take on teaching some of the classes, but I'd have to get at her about that later.

We'd only had a moment to catch up before we started practicing together, but I told him that whatever he wanted to talk about, we'd need to do so after we practiced since we were already running late. The whole time, he was smiling and laughing, and I couldn't have been more embarrassed. Let me do a brief recap. The night he was at my house, he took really good care of me, and I mean, GOOD care of me. Dru fucked me so good that night, I haven't been right ever since, and I haven't been with anyone ever since. There was no way after having a night like that, that you could ever have sex with anyone else the same or even better than that.

The next morning, I made up an excuse as to why he needed to go because I was so embarrassed that I'd acted like a whole complete hoe, but he left me his number. I told myself I wasn't going to call, but after a few months, I finally decided to—seven months later, exactly, and his number was different, so I figured it wasn't meant to be. I could've sent him a DM on Instagram, but some niggas, they fuck and forget. I assumed that would be what would happen, so I never reached back out, and now, here he was right in my face, and I didn't know what to say or how to act.

After we had gotten done with rehearsal for the day, I tried to get away. I wanted to get as far away from him as possible, but that wasn't going to happen because as soon as I started walking away, he grabbed my arm.

"So, you don't know how to use your phone, huh?"

"You don't know how to keep your number the same, huh?"

He turned his head at me. "I'm just wondering when you tried to call to know I changed my number. I had that number for like… most of the year, Christmas. If you wasn't feelin' a nigga—"

I had to stop him. I put my hand over his mouth. "It wasn't that I wasn't feeling you. I had a lot of shit going on. You know Lex, and I had just broken up, we opened this studio—it was a lot going on. I'm sorry for that, but I did think about you. I guess I waited too long."

That was the truth. I had so much going on and even more, and when I reached out to him, it was too late. Maybe me being so guarded really ruined a good thing for me, but who the hell can blame me? Lex literally slept with my best friend, and I didn't and still don't know Dru from any other nigga. I didn't know what he wanted out of life or where he was even trying to go. I knew very little about him, but I was so interested in him. He definitely left a lasting impression. He just didn't know it.

"Ain't no such thing as waiting too long, and obviously fate brought us back together for a reason, so what you tryna do?" He licked his lips and wrapped his arms around my waist. I shouldn't have been so surprised at how bold he was, but that was hard to do. He was making me feel some type of way—the same way he did two years ago.

"Are you still single, because I can't be dealin' with no cheatin' ass—"

"Christmas, I didn't have anybody then, and I don't have anybody now. I ain't been able to get you off my mind for two years. I tried finding you on social media, but you just disappeared. I even asked Blair, and he said he ain't know shit."

"I really was just adjusting and going through some things, but I'm better now—"

"So, then it sound like to me, we good, right?"

"You just gon' cut me off forever? That's what you like to do?"

"Nah, you just talk too much."

I knew I shouldn't, but I really wanted to kiss him. The way he looked and smelled, he had my brain and my panties about to burst. I leaned into him and was about to kiss him when I heard the sweetest voice I'd ever heard. "Mommy! Mommy!"

I let go of Dru, turned around and got down to my knees. Blessing, my daughter, was wobbling into the studio with her hands up, ready for me to kiss all on her.

"There's Mama's baby!"

"Christmas…you…you had a baby?" Dru asked, his voice laced with confusion.

I picked up my baby and turned around.

"Dru, this is Blessing. Blessing, this is your dad."

CHAPTER 6- DRU

I hadn't seen Christmas in so long, and the way she just dropped off the face of the earth, I didn't know if something happened to her or what. Blair even told me she wasn't competing like she used to for a little while. I thought she was still grieving her break up, but it turns out, she was out having a baby. My baby at that. I ain't no fool. Anybody with eyeballs could tell that baby was mine. I wasn't even gon' question if I strapped up that night, because I know I didn't, and I didn't want to. Christmas was so beautiful, and she ain't the type you pull out the protection for. She the type you get pregnant, even though those weren't my intentions.

"You wasn't gon' tell me I had a baby out there?" Anger slowly started seeping its way in once I really got a good look at Blessing.

"Is everything okay?" Kim asked as she approached us. I nodded my head, grabbed Christmas, and took her to the side.

"Did you hear me?" I said that a little more vicious than I meant to, but I meant what I said.

"Listen, Dru, you gotta understand. Initially, no, I didn't think Blessing was your baby. I thought maybe it was Lex's, since he was my boyfriend before you and I had our one-night stand. I wasn't even thinking of the possibility that it could be yours until I got about seven months pregnant. I remembered that Lex and I hadn't really been having sex like that, so I decided to get a DNA test. It came back that Lex wasn't the father. I could deal with his denial and his smart mouth, but I wasn't sure originally if I could deal with yours, so then I tried contacting you when I found out, and I couldn't find you."

"So, you keep a baby from me because you couldn't reach me? My Instagram, Facebook, Twitter, Linked In, and my email address are all broke too?"

"Don't raise your voice at me, Dru. I know you're angr—"

"You damn right I'm angry. I had a whole baby come out of you and you ain't said a word. I can tell the baby is mine. Look at her, Christmas. She look just like me, like I had her by myself. You're foul as fuck for this, and I would've never expected this from you."

I understood where she was coming from, but that didn't mean it hurt any less.

"Dru, I'm sorry. I really am sorry. I wish I could take it back and do it all over again. If I could, I would've told you the truth immediately. I'm sorry, for real."

"Yeah, you are sorry. Give me my baby."

She looked at me like she was about to challenge me. I wouldn't dare put my hands on a female, especially not Christmas because I had some type of feelings for her inside of me, but if she was gon' act like I couldn't hold my own damn daughter, we were about to have a problem. She could tell by the way I was looking at her, I wasn't playing.

Christmas handed me Blessing, and I looked at her. She had the same eyes as me, the same nose, and even the same bone structure, but that smile was just like Christmas'. See, God made me a boxer for a reason—he knew I was gon' have to knock niggas out as an old man over my baby girl one day. I never thought I'd have any kids, not on purpose or on accident, but now that I had one, I'd make the best of it. My father was a good man, and he taught me almost everything I knew. I'd be a good man as well. At thirty years old, it was time for me to slow down.

I was tired of boxing, really just of the wear and tear on my body, and I felt like Blessing was going to be the reason for that slow down.

CHAPTER 7- BLAIR

I saw this about to happen a mile away. I just knew this shit was going to go sour. For the last year, Holiday and I had been dating. She didn't want to call it that, but that's what the fuck it was. She was my bitch, even if she didn't think she was. I had cut off all my hoes for her, which I know concerned her because she thought I couldn't, but for her, I'd do anything.

I met Holiday at a competition some years ago. I had already been following her on social media and baby could dance. Back then, I was still out here hoeing, doing what I wanted, but when I met her during a battle; man, I knew I had to have her. Holiday isn't just pretty, she's fun, and she's got a beautiful personality. She don't like for anybody to know it, but I know she wanna settle down with a nigga, she just scared I'ma treat her like I used to treat other women. I wouldn't do that to Holiday—I couldn't do that to her. She wouldn't allow it, and I wouldn't even give myself the opportunity.

That was also why we were secretly dating. She didn't want to tell anyone, and she didn't want to even admit to me that we were dating or in a relationship. Most nights, she slept at my house, and she was waking up to me. She'd cook in my kitchen, leave her shit at my house, and I even let her drive my car. We was in a full ass relationship. This wasn't my first time at the studio either; I'd been here plenty of times, all the time. When nobody else was here, Holiday and I would fuck all over the furniture, the floor, on the damn dance beam. And she still ain't wanna claim me? You can call me a bitch if you want to, but I love Holiday, and I'm not 'bout to keep on being a secret for something stupid.

Dru and Christmas had walked out after finding out about Blessing. Of course I knew, her auntie was my "girlfriend." I wanted to tell Dru every damn day about what was going on, but it wasn't my place. I didn't want Holiday to feel like I betrayed her trust. I would never do that, even if it was killing me inside, which it was.

Silent, Dakota, Kim and Teddy were gone as well, and it was just me and Holiday, like always.

"So, that was fucked up, huh?" I asked, referring to Blessing.

"I'm just glad it's finally out. Holding in that secret has been haunting me since she told us a year ago. I didn't care who the father was and still don't, but then it's your brother. It's made things kind of weird."

I hoped she wasn't saying this was why she hadn't claimed me or some shit.

"Bae, I'm not John Snow, and you not the Dragon Queen; we ain't blood-related—it's fine."

She busted out laughing, but I was dead ass serious. That man was fucking his auntie. Last time I checked, Holiday wasn't related to me, so it was fine.

"This ain't Game of Thrones period, if we bein' honest. Back up though, you too close."

She put her hands out in front of her, and I was getting sick of this. I hated when she treated me like she didn't even like me for real.

"You done? Ain't no backin' up. Ain't nobody even in here with us, so why you actin' like that?"

I pulled her closer to me, and she was still lookin' around. "Damn, you ashamed of me, Holly?" I called her by the nickname I gave her. Like "Deck the halls with boughs of Holly" type shit.

"Ain't nobody ashamed of you, okay? I was just making sure everyone was gone."

"But why? Please explain to me why the fuck we still sneaking around like some kids? I'm grown, you grown, what is the problem?"

"You don't want to do this right now, Blair. I'm tired, and I've had a long day; I just want to rest."

"Well, I just wanna be able to call the girl I love my fuckin' girlfriend, but I guess we can't always get what the fuck we want, can we?"

"I guess not. Shit, people in hell want ice water, and they just gotta deal with it."

On the inside, I was burning up, and every time we argued like this, she looked even better to me. Holiday turned me on like no other woman ever had, and that shit made me insane. That was another reason I had to cut off all the hoes—there was nobody on this planet who could fuck me like she did. That pussy was like home to me. I didn't want to be with anybody else anyway.

She was in front of me, breathing heavily. Her chest was heaving up and down, and the sweat from her dancing was still sliding in between her breasts. She was so top heavy, I couldn't ignore it. Like magnets, our bodies were drawn together, and I had to have a taste. I started ripping at her clothes, and she tugged at mine. Once I got her shirt off, I put my hand behind her on her back and popped her bra off with one hand. She grinned. Her titties were bouncing in place; her nipples were hard as hell and ready for my mouth.

I got down to my knees and put both of my hands around her titties so I could position them right in the front of my mouth. Her thick, brown nipples always got me rock hard. I could feel my dick swelling up in my pants. Holiday placed her hands in my thick, curly hair and started pulling at it. I already knew what she wanted me to do. My mouth surrounded her nipples, and I sucked hard. As soon as I heard her moan, I knew she was ready.

"Blair, st—stop!" she screamed. This was the way to her heart. Her nipples were swollen, and the heat between us was indescribable.

A few minutes later, I had slob running out of my mouth from sucking so much. Holiday grabbed my face and brought it up to hers, kissing me passionately. She grabbed at my dick. Every time she touched me, the shit almost brought me to my knees. I'm a passionate ass nigga, and I'm sensitive as fuck to touch, I can't help it. My pants were around my ankles, and I was about to take them off when she stopped me.

"No, don't take them off. You been talkin' so much shit about how you can dance circles around me, dance circles in this pussy, with them fuckin' pants on."

My eyebrow went up in satisfaction. I loved when she talked dirty to me. She bent over and pulled her leggings down. I could smell her arousal—shit was loud as fuck, but I didn't care. I loved the smell of that. Her white lace panties were in the way, but I didn't have a problem moving them to the side.

I pushed the small piece of lace over to the side, and I could see the wetness leaking down her leg. I stuck my dick between her legs, rubbing it against her clit and back to the hole, just sticking the tip in.

"Blair, give me my fucking dick!" she shouted.

"Oh, it's your dick now, huh? Say that shit again!" I retorted as I rubbed my dick back against her.

"Baby, please don't play with me. I'm sorry."

"Show me how sorry you are then," I whispered, leaning over to bite her ear. When she turned around and tried grabbing my dick, I put it back in my boxers and pulled my pants up.

"We ain't doin' no more fuckin' 'til you agree to be mine. I love you. You're funny and smart, pretty and driven, and you get me like nobody else ever has. I'm closer to you than I am my own brother, but I can't let you keep treating me like a hoe when I'm tryna lock you down and make you mine. You got a decision to make, and I'm done playing back and forth with you until you do."

I kissed her on the cheek and headed for the door.

Call me a bitch, but I meant what the fuck I said. The ball was in her court, and it was up to her at this point to make the right decision. No matter what, I'd see her tomorrow anyway.

CHAPTER 8- HOLIDAY

Alright, sleeping without the person you're used to sleeping with every night is hard as fuck. I've only had one night of it, and I'm sick to death. Not only did this nigga leave me to have to sleep by myself, but he didn't have sex with me either. That rejection felt real as hell, and I had to make sure I let his ass know that.

The second I woke up, I checked my bed, and when he wasn't there, I was sadder than I'd been in a long time. Blair and I were extremely close, but settling down wasn't something I was sure I could do, especially because we'd been both going our own way for such a long time. He was hoeing, and I was just dating casually, so it wasn't really a thing at first. We were having fun and just enjoying being together. I stayed over most nights with him, and every now and then, he'd come to my house. He was one of the only men I'd ever allowed in my personal space like that, and I cared for him deeply, but I wasn't sure it was meant to be like the movies and shit like that. I wasn't my parents, and everybody's relationship just wasn't that way.

I got up, got in the shower and began washing up. I ran my hands over my body, mad as hell again that I didn't get some of Blair yesterday. He really had the game fucked up, and I was about to let him know just as soon as I got done. I know he thought I was ashamed of him, but for what? He was fine, smart, he had his own career and didn't need to poach mine. Our chemistry was amazing, in and out of the studio, and he made me feel things I'd never felt before. Did I love him? I couldn't say, and I didn't want to talk to my sisters about it. They'd always encouraged me not to date anyone in the industry, the same way I would with them, so I didn't want to say anything and look like a hypocrite. The men in the industry were for everybody; they were all male whores, and I hated them, but Blair, he was different. When we got together, he was willing to change to be with me, but if someone could change all along, why wouldn't they change before I came into their life?

The shit was stressful as fuck.

When I got out of the shower, I went straight to my phone. I scrolled to Blair's name, and I couldn't help but smile when I saw his name. He didn't text me all night, which was unlike him, and it made me wonder if he was mad and how serious he was about this. If he was gonna withhold the dick, I didn't know what I was going to do because baby, that's some good lovin'!

Me: So, this how we doin' it? I could've been over here dead and you wouldn't even know it because you ain't check on me.

B: But it seems like you're fine. You woke up with enough fire to talk crazy to me. Good morning to you too, bae.

I smirked and put my phone down but ended picking it back up because I had more to say to him.

Me: And Idk who you think you are cutting me off. You can't be serious. You can't stay away from me like that.

B: Yet you're the one texting me. I love you, baby. Have a good day, and I'll see you in a few hours.

I got so mad. This man was really burning me up, and what was even worse, was I went to text him back, and my messages turned green.

"This nigga blocked me? Wow!" Talk about being hurt and upset, but I knew if I didn't get it together, I would lose him forever. Something was wrong with me, well, not necessarily. Everybody who isn't ready to commit, it can't be something wrong with them. Maybe committing just wasn't for everybody. I was so confused, and I really wanted to talk to my sisters, but the judgment I felt they would pass on me would make it really hard for me to either talk to Blair again or talk to them about anything else.

I did the only other thing I could do, and that was call my mom. She fell in love with my dad at a time where the industry was different. Maybe she could offer me some advice. Christmas was also always worried about us dating in the industry because people were always pulling publicity stunts. Nobody has time to be having their relationship taken as a joke because nobody trusts or believes you're in a real one.

As I was putting on my clothes, I scrolled to my mom's name and took a deep breath.

"Good morning, 'Day. What ya doin', baby?"

"Mommy, I need some advice."

"Anything for you, baby. Go ahead..."

CHAPTER 9- SILENT

I decided to come to the studio before everyone else to get a jump on practice for Kim's wedding. I couldn't wait until the day I got married to have my big day, and it all be about me. Now, this next part gon' make me sound like a hater, but I love my sisters, let me say that now. However, Christmas is the oldest, and she's always been in tune and on point with the dance moves. If it wasn't for her, I don't know if either of us would have fallen in love with dance as much if it weren't for her. Holiday was funny and pretty; she had a life outside of dance, and she was always the popular one that everybody liked. Then, there's me, the baby sister of two of the best dancers in the world. The daughter to award-winning dancers and I'm a little on the thick side; this world has been cold.

That was another reason why I had to come in here today to get it right. The entire world was either always looking at me or never looking at me, and it was never for the right reasons. I was about to get shit right for this wedding though, I knew that. I also wanted to come in early today because I couldn't stop thinking about Christmas and Blessing and how I hoped that went over well. I figured if Christmas came in early enough, we could talk about everything going on with her and Dru or if anything was going on at all.

I know he shouldn't have been, but Dakota was crossing my mind. I couldn't stop thinking about how big and strong he was and what his arms felt like around me. I went with that feeling and decided to cut the music on and start to dance. I just wanted to warm up first, and then I'd get into the routine. I closed my eyes and let my body go with the music. It felt so good to just move around the floor without any worries or cares. Dakota popped back into my mind, and his smile was warm and bright—the way dancing made me feel. Whenever I danced, I felt like I was in a room all by myself, like I was doing my own thing.

I moved across the floor, my arms flowing freely. I was breathing hard as hell, but not in exhaustion, more so in excitement. Three minutes later, the music ended, and I had slid across the floor. When I opened my eyes, I was chest to chest with Dakota. I just knew I had to be dreaming when I opened my eyes, and he was staring right at me.

"What you doin' here?"

"Honestly, I wanted to prove to Kim I could be on time. I didn't think you'd be here too."

I raised my lips. This sounded like a whole ass lie.

"You didn't know I would be here, but you came to the back to do what exactly?"

"Practice. I know we got a little time before everybody's supposed to be here. I also wanted to impress you, as well. I wanted to keep my word, so I could leave with your number today."

He was gon' leave with something today alright with the way he was looking. His big, fine ass was wearing this v-neck black t-shirt and these basketball shorts that hugged his thighs in the right place. Lord have mercy.

"Well, lucky for you, I'm ready to dance. Show me what you got."

I opened my arm, ready to lead him, but he proved me wrong. As soon as the music started, he was standing on the right side of me, with his hands up the way they were supposed to be. I didn't have to fix his posture or his legs like I did the day before. I guess he really was ready.

"So, I'ma get that number?" he asked, looking over at me into my eyes. He was staring at me so hard, or it felt so good to have him looking at me like that, that I completely missed my cue.

"I'll start the song over."

He laughed, but it wasn't funny. I'd never met anyone that made me feel like this before. Being here with him now had my insides turning upside down, but it also just felt good to be in the company of another man.

The music began again, and I started counting for us.

"1, 2 3 & 4, 1, 2 3 & 4."

He was hitting all the movements perfectly, and I, for one, was definitely amazed by this.

"You went home and practiced?" I smiled.

"I did. I meant what I said yesterday, and I intend on getting it."

Something about the way he said 'getting it' sounded different in my head, and I didn't see any point in waiting. I pulled him down to me mid-step and kissed him. He slipped his tongue into my mouth, and just like I thought it would, it swept me off my feet. I'd only known this man...not even twenty-four hours, and that kiss was like nothing else in this world...well, it was close to something. It made me feel like I was dancing. When I opened my eyes, I was across the room.

"How did I get over here?"

"We were still moving to the music; you just light on ya feet."

That was something I'd never heard before. As he was looking down into my eyes, Dakota's beard was tickling my face. He backed up a bit and said, "My bad, I didn't mean to tickle you."

"You sure about that?"

I turned around to walk away, and he said loud enough for only me to hear, "You keep on playin' with me, I'ma tickle something else."

"Prove it," I mouthed. I didn't think he'd really be about it, but you know what they say, expect the unexpected. I was headed into the bathroom of the studio when I felt Dakota's strong hands wrap around my waist. He bent down and started kissing the nape of my neck, moving my hair out of the way at the same time. I breathed in deep; this was exactly what I needed.

Dakota pushed me into the bathroom and flipped the lock on the door.

"What you doin'?" I asked in between breaths.

"About to give you what you need, and when I'm done, you gon' give me more than your number."

"Shit, like what?"

"Shhh...."

Dakota whispered. I went to turn the light off, and he grabbed my arm. "I wanna see all of you, not just some of you, and not just a little bit. I wanna see everything."

My heart was racing. I wasn't ashamed of my body, but I was surprised at what he was asking. At this point, he could have my skin if he wanted it because I was about to explode.

Dakota put his hands around my ass and lifted me up, placing me on the sink like I was nothing but a twig. I liked that shit. Ravenously, we began kissing as if we were each other's last meals. I could feel the heat between my legs rising like the mercury was about to run out of the thermometer. I started trying to take my clothes off, and Dakota grabbed my hands. "Let me do that shit. Sit there and look good," he growled. I immediately put my hands at my side. Whatever he said at this point, I would do.

Instead of removing my shirt, he pulled at my breasts, pulling them both out at the same time. He was licking and sucking on them wildly. His tongue kept brushing up against my nipples, and the shit was driving me wild. I had my legs wrapped around his waist, but they kept sliding down, and I guess he took that as his cue to lick my pussy. When his head started traveling down my body, my breasts flopped over the top of my shirt. Dakota moved away from the sink and pulled at my pants.

"Damn, no panties?" He licked his lips, and his eyes got dark, like he was hungrier than he'd ever been. I wasted no time scooting down to the edge of the sink and tilting my pelvis up. That did me no good because all he did was use his strength to pull me down further to wrap my legs around his neck. He was now on his knees and ready to devour me. I could literally feel my pussy thumping, and my heartbeat was raging through my ears.

As soon as he put his tongue on my pussy, my body started vibrating. It had been too long since I'd been touched by somebody that wasn't me.

"Fuck! Dakota!"

His head was moving so fast in between my legs, I knew he would pound this pussy like a psycho would. My left leg had gone numb he was eating so good, and the macaroni sound was the loudest thing in the room. Shit was crazy. Right before I was about to cum, he rose to his feet and undid his pants. His dick fell out of his boxers like a snake trying to get free, and I touched my stomach. I knew my ovaries were about to get rearranged, amen!

He pulled me closer to him and groaned, "I want you to cum on this dick."

I wasn't going to say no to that, at all. Especially not since his dick was practically growing at the sight of me. Dakota slid into me, and I could feel the pressure all the way in my ass. The shit was amazing. The thrusts were slow and steady at first, but the more our orgasms started to build, the faster he went. Dakota picked me up and slammed my back against the wall.

"Uhn!" I screamed, realizing it made the dick slide in even further. Dakota bounced me on his dick as I used the wall to help him, because I'm not lazy, and the shit was about to take me out.

"Damn, this some good ass pussy, Silent. Don't be quiet, talk to me."

"It...feels...soooo...good, Dakota. Don't stop!"

Meanwhile, I was the one saying not to stop, but I'd already leaked out so much juice onto him This wasn't going to work. My eyes were rolling in the back of my head. I couldn't hold on much longer.

"Uhn-huh, stay with me, sexy. That pussy too good for you to be passin' out on me."

I laughed as he kept bouncing me up and down. I put my arms around his neck and squeezed tighter, holding on for dear life.

"Fuck!" Dakota yelled out. I knew everyone else in the building could hear him, but I didn't give a fuck. My insides were being beat out, and just when I thought I couldn't take anymore, because I couldn't, he pulled out, and his shiny and glistening dick leaked all over my stomach. We were both breathing hard as hell, and I'd never felt so out of control, but I loved it.

"Thank you for that. It's been a long time."

"It don't have to be another wait in your life, for real."

"You'll call me when this is over today?"

"Run me them digits, baby."

I loved the way he talked. His fine big ass. He pulled out his phone, and I put my number inside. "Now, you ready to go dance for real? Everyone should be waiting for us."

"Let 'em wait a minute more."

Dakota grabbed me, wrapped his arms around me one more time, and we shared another kiss.

CHAPTER 10- CHRISTMAS

Arriving at the dance studio, my nerves were a damn wreck. Yesterday, Dru and I didn't argue, and he didn't really talk crazy to me, but he was mad as hell. I didn't know how this was going to affect his sister's wedding, whom I'd grown somewhat attached to after speaking with her and helping to come up with a routine for her wedding. Not to mention she's Blessing's aunt. What I did was wrong, and I didn't mean for it to come out like this. Maybe I didn't mean for it to at all. I don't really know.

He was so upset, and he had every right to be. I'd never been more upset at myself for not saying something when I knew I should have. I couldn't believe I did this to him, to myself, and to Blessing. He'd already missed so many firsts, and it wasn't because she didn't have a father but because I kept him away from her. I should have done more. I should have been better.

When I arrived at the dance studio, I was glad I had Blessing in the backseat, because the moment I got out of the car, I saw Dru pulling up. He had the sternest look on his face, and I knew I was about to get a mouth full. I was heading to open the car door, when he jogged over and grabbed my hand.

"I got it. You already know I don't play that opening the door shit."

"She's a baby, Dru. I think it's okay."

"You might, but it isn't. You should never have to open a door, and my daughter damn sure won't either."

I understood, and I knew his hostility in what he was saying didn't take away from what he actually thought and how he felt.

I moved away from the door and let him get her out. I grabbed her bag, and he also took that from me.

"Man, I don't get why you don't get it yet; you don't need to touch anything but yourself. You kept me away from my baby all this time, and all I want to do is spend as much time with her as I possibly can. I want to be a gentleman to you as well. I already know that shit you went through with Lex got you fucked up. That's why you don't wanna let me be in your life for real, and that's fine, but when I am around, I'ma treat you like the woman you deserve to be treated like. Accept it or don't, but I'm not 'bout to keep having this conversation with you. Who's gonna watch Blessing when it's time to dance?"

I was so lost in everything he was saying, it took me a minute to answer. "She's going to sit with the receptionist, Michelle. She's her regular babysitter."

"Straight like that. Come on so we can get this shit over with."

I didn't like how he was talking to me, but I understood where he was coming from. I deserved it, for sure. When we got to the door, even with the baby in his hands, he opened the door up and held it for me, and then came in behind me. I walked him over to the receptionist's desk, and he handed Michelle his baby, but not before kissing her on the cheek.

"You're really good with her, you know?"

He nodded his head. I'd been watching him, and the way she received him, and how she looked at him. They were clearly already bonding, something I knew all about. I loved my daddy, and I couldn't imagine growing up without him.

"I bet I could've been even better had I been here this whole time."

His bitching was getting old, and I wasn't about to let him keep talking to me like this.

"Look, I know you're mad, and I'm sorry about not telling you. I'm sorry I didn't try harder to find you, and I know I should have, but you can't keep talking to me like this. Either we gon' get over it and learn to co-parent together, or we not, but either way, you gon' have to show me some respect."

He turned around and looked at me like he wanted to go off. Instead, he nodded his head and just walked through the double doors to meet everyone else. I didn't know how to make things between us better, but this wasn't going to work if we weren't both trying to make it better.

When we got inside, Silent looked like someone had just beat her up, like she'd been rolling around on the ground or like she'd already gotten a really good workout.

"You good, sis?"

"I've never actually been better. I'm ready. Where's everyone else?"

"We're here!" Kim sang as she and Teddy came in. They were such a cute couple, and I could tell they were really in love. Blair came in behind them, and not even five minutes later, Holiday was coming in as well.

"Alright, we've only got a few more days left, and I think we need to stay as long as we need to, to get it done!" I shouted as I got the music together. I didn't know what was wrong, but I could tell something was off with Blair and Holiday. I stopped the music and went to the back.

"Whatever the issue is between you two, I'ma need y'all to fix it. Yesterday, it seemed like the chemistry between y'all was good, and now…things don't seem right, so what y'all gon' do?"

Holiday rolled her eyes and walked away, and Blair apologized.

"It's me. I'm not feeling well today, and I think she's getting upset about it. I'll be alright, and I'll get it together."

"Everybody better. Neither one of y'all niggas better not ruin my day, especially not you, 'Kota!" Kim shouted.

"Good. Everybody, let's get to work."

I could feel the anger radiating off of Dru's body, but we were going to be okay, at least I hoped we would.

"You know, it's not that you didn't tell me. I'm mad for real for real about some shit that happened before that technically. I'm mad because you waited seven months to even try and reach out to me. You was already pregnant, but you wasn't checkin' for me before that."

"That's not true. I—"

"Nope, don't even say anything else. It don't even matter. Let's just figure out how to work this shit out for Blessing, and then, we can be done with one another."

Wow, that hurt way more than I thought it would. I didn't

want to completely lose him, not like this anyway, but I had to make sure the steps were perfect for Kim and her special day.

CHAPTER 11- BLAIR

I went after Holiday because at this point, she was acting like a brat, and I couldn't take it anymore. I followed her outside, and she was sitting on top of her car. I knew she couldn't be acting like this over no dick.

"So, you mad because I wouldn't fuck you last night?"

"No, boy. Yo' dick ain't that good!" She rolled her eyes and sucked her teeth, but I couldn't tell by the way she was acting.

"Listen, I've been up front and honest with you about how I feel. I'm not about to keep on giving you free dick when I'm not getting anything in return."

"So, you think I'm a prostitute now?" Holiday slid off of the car and walked up to me with her arms folded.

"That's not what I said. What I said was I'm willing to give you my all, to love you and be there for you, and I can't see you really wanting to do the same. I'm not about to keep on sharing my body with someone who don't take me seriously."

"This shit is beyond me, Blair! It really is. When I met you, you were fuckin' this girl and this girl, living your best life, and now, you don't want to do that same thing? That really is blowing my mind. Why you wanna go and ruin things?"

"Ruin them? You know what? I'm done, and this time, I mean like done-done. You ain't even gotta worry about me. That's what's wrong with chicks like you. A nigga who wanna change, does change, and tries to fall in love and be happy with their bitch, and they don't even wanna let 'em. Let Kim know that when the day comes, I'll be ready, but I don't wanna see yo' ass 'til then, and I mean that shit!"

I left her stupid ass standing in the parking lot. I didn't even need this practice for real. I was only here because I knew it would make Kim happy, and I'd be able to see Holiday in a setting outside of home. I needed to be with someone who wasn't ashamed of me, and that wasn't her.

When I got in the car, I heard my phone ringing. I pulled it out of my pocket, looked at it, and it was my mom. A smile quickly crept its way up onto my face. I hadn't talked to her in a few days. She was busy helping Kim with her wedding, and she really was good at this stuff too.

"Hey, Mama. What's up?"

"Hey, baby. I was calling to see how everything is going?"

"What you mean, Mama? Kim's dance rehearsal stuff is good. You probably know more about what's going on with the wedding than I do."

"That's not what I'm talking about, baby. Is everything okay with you? God dropped it off in my spirit that something was wrong."

Man, a mother's intuition really was no joke. I had already told my mom about Holiday before, and I was tired of talking 'bout it because I felt stupid about her not wanting to be with me.

"Man, Ma, it's Holiday—"

"Again? You sure that girl is worth all the chasing?"

I laughed because a part of me wasn't, but there was that other part of me that was.

"Mama, you told me that when you met Dad, you knew he was the one, and I feel the same way. I know Holiday is the one for me, but she's scared to settle down. I think she thinks I'm going to change or go back to doing what I was before her, but she completes me, Mama. She's the one, but I don't know what else to do."

As I drove, I felt pain in my heart, real pain. I don't care what nobody say, when you in love and the person you love won't do right, that shit will fuck with you. And I love me some Holiday.

"Well, times ain't the same as they used to be, and that's just the truth, but if you love this girl and you think she loves you too, why not propose? Why not give her a grand gesture? You done did everything else you can do, baby. Either take the leap or walk away."

My mom was right. It had been a year, and I'd been into her from day one. I wanted to be with her from day one. I loved her, and there was no way I could just let her go like that, but she needed some time to cool down, and so did I.

"Thanks for the advice, Ma. Hopefully, I don't make a fool out of myself if I decide to."

"Hopefully, not. Remember, you're a prize too, not just her."

"I love you, Ma."

"Love you too, Blair. Talk to you soon."

Damn, I loved my mama.

CHAPTER 12- DAKOTA

It was the day of Kim's wedding. I thought it was interesting that she wanted to get married right before it got cold. I assumed she'd want to get married when it got cold since the snow would've made a winter wonderland type of situation, and she was just like a princess. But if she was happy, so was I, and I couldn't have been happier.

The gym was doing great, and I was getting new members all the time. Plus, Silent was making sure a nigga stayed good. We had been talking for the last several days, every day, all day long. We FaceTimed, texted, and talked on the phone all day. Even when she was in the middle of doing her classes, she had me in her headphones the whole time, and baby had me going.

We decided that not only would we be partners but that she would be my date to the wedding, and I couldn't wait to see her. I hadn't seen her outside of dance rehearsal, but I knew she was going to be beautiful, and I was missing them guts, just to be honest. I parked the car, stepped out, and called her to see where she was. Even I had to take a second to admire the wedding venue because Sis really had her wedding shit together. I called Silent to see where she was, but before it even connected, she was pulling up. I walked over to her door and opened it up. When she got out, she looked amazing. She didn't need to change her clothes until it was time for the reception, and baby was wearing the fuck out of the dress she had on, too.

"I'm sayin' though, do a little spin for me, why don't you."

I grabbed her hand, and she spun around. Her ass was lookin' good and so was everything else. She wore a deep red dress with long sleeves, and it fit her perfectly. Her shoes were deep red and black, and her hair was up in a bun with bangs that feel just over her face. She was beautiful.

"You ready to go inside?" she asked, smoothing out her dress.

"I'm ready to take you in the back of the car to be real, but if you ready to go inside, then we gon' do what you want."

"That's all you think about, ain't it?"

Looking at her here and now, it was true; I did think about the sex a lot. I mean, that pussy was hittin', but I loved how beautiful she was, and I'm not talking about just the physical—she really had a beautiful soul. I've seen a lot of stuff, and I've connected with a lot of energy, but something about her was different. Maybe it was the age difference. She was only twenty-three, but she made my old ass feel young, had me staying up all night tryna text and talk to her all the time. She had me feelin' like a lil' girl for real.

"Nah, that ain't all I think about, but you have been recently. You got everything you need?"

She grabbed her bag from the back seat and said, "I do now. Thank you for asking me to be your date."

"Thank you for having me. Come on."

I grabbed her hand and helped her walk across the gravel parking lot—not that she needed my help, but I wanted everybody to see my baby on my arm. I didn't want there to be any question about who she was or what she was doing. When we walked up the stairs to get to the venue, we could see people coming in and out of the door, smiling, with drinks in their hands. It reminded me of a crowded restaurant with people moving around so much. I saw some of the people we'd grown up with, and I spoke. Everyone wanted to know who the woman on my arm was, and that feeling was straight. I had never brought anyone around my family.

"I guess you weren't lying. Everybody keeps asking me who I am like they didn't know you like girls or something."

"Don't say that gay shit. They know I like girls. What they didn't know was that I was interested in somebody."

"Somebody, or me?" Her eyebrows went up in confusion as she grabbed a glass of champagne off one of the waiter's trays.

"You, baby, you. Don't act brand new."

"I'm not. I just wanted to make sure we were on the same

page."

"Same page? Baby, we in the same book. I told you what it was already. I'm not getting any younger, I'm tired of sleeping around, and I damn sure don't want to be runnin' around town with different women. I'm ready to settle down, and meeting you couldn't have come at a better time."

She tossed the champagne back, swallowed it and then put her arms around me. "You're exactly right because I wanted the same thing. We still have a long way to go, and I hope we make it to the finish line."

"What would be the finish line for you, baby?" I placed my hands on her hips, squeezing them. She had a little extra meat right there, and I loved that shit.

"Long term relationship, marriage type shit. You know."

"I can dig it, baby. Now, Ms. Silent, would you please allow me to escort you to our seats?"

"I told you to stop doing that accent shit. You ain't a butler, and it's not funny."

"Yet, you're smiling." I flashed her my teeth, letting her see all thirty-two.

"That's because you make me smile and you make me feel passion. Is it a crime, 'Kota?"

"One day, loving you might be. Squash that 'Kota shit. I just want you to call me baby."

We both busted out laughing and headed inside one of the ballrooms where the actual wedding was going to be held. I could legit get used to some shit like this.

"Honestly, I'm disappointed, and I don't know what else to tell you." Christmas shrugged her shoulders. It was hard for me to hear that my sister, who was also my best friend, was disappointed in me.

"I'm not tryna disappoint you, Christmas. I mean, what else do you want me to say?"

"I just want you to slow down. That partying shit is dead. Thank God you at least know who the father is. It is Blair, right?"

"How'd you know?" I asked, truly shocked. I hadn't told anyone about me and Blair.

"Do you think I'm stupid? You been runnin' around here sneaking like a maniac, canceling hangouts, and not to mention, I can see everything on the security footage. Why didn't you tell me? Does Silent know, and I don't?"

"Slow down, Rambo. I haven't told anybody about the baby, that's one thing. Mom knows about Blair, because I called her to get some advice, but I didn't feel comfortable using the advice. At least not when I should've used it, I guess. Now Blair is pissed off and won't talk to me. He stormed off from me the other day, but I haven't heard from him since."

Christmas sat down beside me and grabbed my hand. I found out I was pregnant two days ago. Something inside of me just didn't seem right, and I didn't know what it was, but something told me to get a pregnancy test. I wasn't sick, I didn't not feel good. I just felt…shit, I felt like an alien had invaded my damn body, and I was right! I was carrying Blair's baby, and I couldn't even tell him because he didn't want to talk to me.

"Do not make the same mistake I made, Holiday. Do you hear me? I don't know if Dru and I will ever be okay after this. But you and Blair have a chance to make it right, and I really want to see that happen between you two, you understand?"

My head damn near fell in my lap. This was hard for me to be going through. We had the Christmas shows coming up, not to mention just my career, and I hadn't talked to Blair. I didn't want to lose him, and I knew with something like this, I might actually push him away. I'd been running from him for so long, would he actually want to still be with me?

"I love Blair, but I don't know. I don't want things to change between us. It's so..."

"Easy because you're not in a committed relationship? It might seem easier, but by doing things this way, you accidentally fell in love, and you've been hurting someone else along the way. You've become everything you hate, 'Day. That sound right to you?"

"Dammmnnn, just read me, why don't you?"

"I'm your big sister; it's my job. Now, we done in this fancy ass bathroom? I gotta get back to my own dramatic life, and you need to go and talk to Blair. I know he's running around here somewhere already."

We both stood up from the couch in the bathroom and hugged. There was a loud knock on the door. Both of us froze and looked toward it.

"Holiday, I know you didn't lock that damn door. You too damn old to be doin' shit like that!"

"Uhn-uhn, I don't want them people in my business. They're alright; this can't be the only damn bathroom."

We both laughed, and Christmas shook her head at me. I was being dead ass serious that I didn't want anyone in my business. I was already pregnant by a dancer. Lord, the world's biggest stereotype, but I did love and care about Blair, and it was time that I showed him.

I unlocked the bathroom door, and Christmas and I came out giggling. There were women trying to get in the bathroom and who knows how long they'd been waiting. Christmas grabbed my hand, gave it a light squeeze, and gave me a knowing look. I nodded my head and went to find Blair. There was only about thirty minutes before the wedding, so he should've been here already,

ready to stand in his place for Ted, since he was one of his grooms-men.

I traveled down three extremely long ass hallways, and still, I didn't find Blair. There was about fifteen minutes left before the wedding started, and I didn't want to be in the way. We'd all been invited as guests, and I didn't want to be the sore thumb sticking out. I was about to head into the ballroom to take my seat when I smelled something that was unmistakable as anything else other than Blair. Something about that Gucci cologne would travel through my nose and straight through my body. I turned around and he looked so damn good. We'd had a few fights previously, but this was the worst one ever. Him not giving me any sex, not talking to me, and then showing up like this looking all sexy in an all-white tuxedo with the red tie. Lord, hold me.

Immediately, our eyes connected, and I couldn't stop staring at him. He smirked, and we both started walking toward one another at the same time.

"You look—"

"No, baby, you look beautiful. I mean…damn."

He grabbed my arm and spun me around, taking a good look at my body.

"Thank you, Blair. I, uhm…I need to talk to you about something."

"I do, too. Come over here with me."

He grabbed my hand and led me out of the crowded room. "What's going on?"

There was a bench in the hallway, and we decided to take a seat. I didn't know what was going on, but I felt like for some reason in my soul, this was about to be the end of us.

"So, you know how I feel about you. I love you for real, Holiday, and I don't care if you think it hasn't been enough time or if you—"

"I love you too, Blair, and I'm sorry it took me so long to say it."

I could tell by the shocked look on his face, he wasn't expecting to hear that today or at least not right now, but I did love him, with all my heart.

"I wasn't prepared to hear that, but just hold that thought, and let me finish, so you can take the whole wedding to think about what I'm about to say if you need to."

I perked up and really started listening. "I love you, Holiday, and I have since I first laid eyes on you. Watching you dance is legit like watching an angel come down from heaven. I don't care what happened in the past or what you're used to. All I care about is us moving forward, and that's what I really want. I want to make you mine forever and only mine. I know you haven't been with anyone else, and I been too busy runnin' after your ass to be with anybody. I'm ready to take it to the next level, fuck dating. I wanna make you my wife."

Blair slid down from the bench and onto one knee. I grabbed at my chest, just knowing he wasn't about to do this.

"You are my life, and my world. Will you marry me?"

Blair pulled out a tiny white box, and when he opened it, I could've hit the ground.

"Blair!" I shouted. I couldn't contain the feelings I had inside of me. Everything was telling me to say yes, but I needed him to know about the baby first. I didn't want him thinking I was just marrying hm to trap him or something. I didn't want him feeling like I didn't think he deserved me.

"Before I say yes, I need to tell you something, Blair. I found out a few days ago, I'm pregnant."

Blair's hands dropped to his side, and I just knew this was the end.

"I just wanted to be honest and tell you."

"Man, this is the best fucking news I've ever gotten in my life!"

Blair jumped off the ground and picked me up off the bench, spinning me around.

"Blair, put me down!"

"Hell nah, I'm never letting you go, and you can go ahead and say yeah. I'm not bringing no baby of mine into the world unless I make his mother an honest woman, so give me your hand."

I couldn't laugh or even say no. Tears were pouring down my face as I stuck my hand out. Blair slid that ring on, and I swear I felt like a shift occur. Like something in my life had suddenly just changed. The ring was so nice; it wasn't a diamond—he instead got me my favorite, a sapphire. He said it was colorful and different like me. I didn't see this coming before this day, but now that it was happening, I couldn't have been happier.

Together, we walked into the ballroom, and as soon as I took a seat with Christmas and Silent, I had to put them up on game.

"Excuse me, excuse me, Mrs. Gains coming through." I stuck my hand out in front of them, and they both started squealing.

"Shh…people 'bout to start comin' in."

They were both drooling over my hand, and I loved the attention. Then I thought about Silent, and I didn't want her to feel left out. I started to open my mouth when she held up her hand. "Girl, I already know. I saw y'all in the studio, and Christmas just told me the rest."

"Well damn, just tell everybody my business, why don't you?" I laughed at Christmas.

"Silent ain't everybody, she's our sister, and secrets are what is destroying us. We gotta be willing to just break down and tell the truth."

I could hear the conviction in my sister's voice, and it hurt me to see her feeling so sad and down. I hoped that she'd be able to fix things with Dru. If I could fix things with Blair, surely, they'd be okay.

CHAPTER 14- DRU

The wedding was beginning, and all I could do was look at Christmas. Man, she had me so damn mad, but I knew I needed to cool out. I couldn't keep giving her the cold shoulder like this. Over the last few days, she had been letting me spend time with Blessing, but even when I was with her, I wouldn't say much to Christmas. During the rehearsals, there wasn't really much for me to say, and I didn't want to say the wrong thing, so I stayed quiet. Now looking at her, my heart fluttered for her. I wished I wasn't so damn prideful, but she really had me fucked up, keeping a whole child away from me. That's some bullshit.

I shook the thoughts out of my head as Kim walked down the aisle with our dad. She looked so beautiful, and she had tears coming down her face. Teddy was her soulmate and her true love. I couldn't say Christmas was that for me, but I definitely had some type of feelings for her, especially now that she had my baby.

Kim came down the aisle and joined hands with Teddy. I looked behind me and saw Blair's face; he had tears in his eyes, ole sensitive ass. Then I looked at Dakota, who was sitting in the front pew with our mom, looking proud as ever. This day really changed my life and brought us all together, even Blair and his weird fling with Holiday. Even if he thought we didn't know, we all knew. He got to be smarter than that.

Kim and Teddy said their I do's a lot quicker than I expected. I wanted to prolong this reception at all costs because the dancing situation was about to take me out. I ain't really wanna be bothered with Christmas for real, but I had to do what I had to do.

When the nuptials were over, we headed into the back to change our clothes and then get ready to dance. It was the opening of the actual reception and people were still being seated. Christmas and I stood next to one another once we were done changing. Neither of us said a word, not at first anyway, but I decided to be the one to break the ice.

"Where's Blessing?"

"With my mom."

"Mm..."

"Mmmm what, Dru?" She turned around and faced me with her arms folded across her chest. I didn't say anything. I wasn't in the mood for arguing, and this shit was getting old. Finally, the music started, and on cue, all of us together began coming in in a straight line, prepared to dance our lives away. The crowd clapped and cheered, and everybody was happy and excited. The dancing part was actually fun. It was looking Christmas so close in the face that was hard because we weren't seeing eye to eye.

By the time the dance was over, we were both sweaty and ready to change our clothes again, but I wasn't sure if she was staying. "You stayin' for the reception?"

"If I do, is that a problem?"

"Nah, I just wanted to—"

"Hey, hey, hey, beautiful. I'm sorry to interrupt, but the way you were moving out there—"

"No, my nigga, you ain't sorry to interrupt, but you gon' be sorry if you don't step the fuck off!" I shouted. Niggas was rude as hell. I know he saw me standing right here, not only talking to her, but just a few minutes ago, we were just making love to music with our movements, so I couldn't get with dude.

"Oh, this you?" he asked, pointing at me, talking to Christmas. Before she could even say a word, I stood in front of her and put my arms around her. "This answer your question, nigga?" I squeezed her as tight as I could and put my lips to hers. At first, I did it because I didn't want this nigga talkin' to her, but then, it was just like before. We fell back into kissing like it was nothing. By the time the dude walked away, I decided to pull away from her.

"What was that?" she asked. I couldn't even respond. This shit was about to make me crazy. All I could do was walk away. My mind was racing, and I didn't know what to do anymore, and Christmas' fine ass was ruining me, I swear.

CHAPTER 15

Three months later

It's beginning to look a lot like CHRISTMAS

"Blessing, don't touch that!" I shouted as Blessing ran through the living room. It was Christmas Eve, and I decided to let Blessing open up her gifts early because she was little and didn't have any siblings. Not to mention, tonight was one of our biggest shows. I knew tomorrow I would be tore up, and Christmas was going to give me a headache. I needed to be able to sleep in.

Since the wedding, Dru had been over here everyday to see Blessing, so he said. He said it didn't have a damn thing to do with me, but I don't know if I can agree with that or not. Since he kissed me at the wedding, he's been overprotective, super crazy, and just being loud with me all the time. He's acting like I'm his girlfriend. I tried to get him to forgive me for keeping Blessing a secret, and he said he did, but I couldn't tell, not at all.

I had just finished wrapping all of her gifts just to let her tear them all the hell up. She deserved it though—Blessing was my only baby, and I intended to spoil her with everything inside of me, no matter what that meant. I wanted her to have my time and attention, my love and affection, and anything else on this planet that she could possibly ever want.

"Come here, baby. Come here!" She waddled over to me, and I pulled her in between my legs so we could start opening her presents. She had a whole living room full of stuff, and it would take us quite a while to get everything open. I didn't tell Holiday or Silent I was going to be opening her gifts with her early because I wanted it to be something special. My parents and her aunties could give them whatever they were going to give her tomorrow, and Dru and I hadn't even discussed Christmas. All of this was brand new to both of us. I didn't want to ask him to come over because he'd been here everyday and was really trippin', so I deserved a little peace before tonight.

I reached for one of Blessing's small toys, and then the door-bell went off. I just knew it was Dru before I got up. Not to mention I could see through the glass and see the silhouette of his body. I picked Blessing up off the floor, not wanting her to choke on the wrapping paper or anything else and went to open the door. Dru was standing there with two handfuls of gifts.

"Can I come in? It's cold, snowing, and you got my baby all in the door. You want her to get sick?"

"Sounds like you don't want to get sick, but yes, come in."

I moved out the way to let him in the house. He put the bags on the floor and started taking off his shoes. "What you doin'?"

"I came so my baby could open her gifts. I have a last minute match tomorrow, and I'm leaving town."

"Leaving town? So, you weren't coming to my Christmas show tonight?" I didn't know why I was so offended, but I was. I just automatically assumed he would come.

"Why would I come? It's not like you invited me, and other than seeing my daughter, I didn't think we were in that place with one another."

"You know what?" I said as I put Blessing down. I didn't want her to hear what I was about to say to her father. "You kiss me at your sister's wedding because somebody else was trying to talk to me. You come over here everyday to "see Blessing" even though she's sleep most of the time, but you didn't think you were invited to Christmas show? Get the fuck out of here, Dru. I would have never expected this from you, and it hurts me to know that you don't give a fuck about how I'm feel—"

My words were stopped by his hands squeezing my ass and his lips touching mine. Like a bad habit, I put my arms around his neck and let him kiss me, as deeply as he wanted to. God, this man was so addictive. We stood there kissing for what seemed like for-ever, and then he moved.

"Look, I wanted to talk to you about all this shit. I was wrong as hell for treating you the way I have the last several months. I been poppin' up whenever I want to, talking to you crazy, all types of shit, but it's because I don't wanna lose you to another nigga, not while you raisin' my daughter. I don't know what you've got goin' on for yourself and your life other than dance, of course, but you kicked me out of your life, and I been actin' childish as fuck for that."

I couldn't believe he was saying this to me, but it was nice to hear. "So, what you sayin'?"

"I'm saying I'm done acting stupid, and if I would have known you wanted me to come to your Christmas show, I would've made other arrangements."

I stepped away from him and smiled. "Well, make other arrangements. I do want you there, Dru."

"Say less. You forgive me?"

"I'm mad, and I don't really want to because you been actin' insane, but yes, I forgive you. All I ask is that you keep doing what you've been doing by being good to our daughter, okay?"

"You ain't gotta tell me that, and the only thing I'ma ask of you is not to be talkin' to no other dudes. Since I'm back now, after long enough, don't let me catch you with somebody else, Christmas. I thought about you for two years too long, waiting for you to call and tryna find you and I couldn't. Now that I have, I just wanna raise our baby together and be happy, but just you and me."

I understood that completely because that was how I was feeling. I wanted to see where things between me and Dru could go. I knew he had a lot of potential, and the feelings were mutual between us. Having Blessing could only bring us closer together, and I couldn't wait for that. Dru went to pick up Blessing and then pulled out his phone to make arrangements for him to be in the city tomorrow so he could fight his match. He said he wanted to support me tonight, and I was glad that he changed his mind and wanted to go.

"Alright, who's ready to open up some presents?" Dru asked. Blessing started wiggling around in his arms, throwing her hands up. She already knew what time it was, and this moment was like no other.

Dru, Blessing, and I spent the rest of the day together, and we even rode to the show together as well. It was almost midnight, and the show would start directly at 12:01. One of my favorite things about the Christmas shows were the announcers, but what nobody knew this year, was they were going to let me do it. I had a special shout out to make now anyway.

When we got downtown to the building where the biggest Christmas show in the USA would take place, I had Dru drop me off in the front, and I gave him the extra tickets I had for him to sit with my parents. We always had extra tickets just in case other people wanted to show up. I immediately went to the back and found my sisters, who were gossiping away. I didn't want to interrupt them. I instead went ahead and got ready for the show. It took me thirty minutes or so to finish up, but now, I was ready to dance.

Behind the curtain, I held Christmas and Silent's hands, knowing we were all proud of one another. A man came up behind me, one of the stagehands, and put a mic around my head.

"What's going on, Christmas?" Silent asked.

"You'll see, just watch. I love you, sisters."

They smiled, and we made our way onto the stage. The crowd went crazy. The clock was counting down, and the ten seconds between Christmas Eve and Christmas quickly changed.

"Merry Christmas, everyone!" I said to the crowd. They cheered and then took their seats.

"Each year, we gather here to watch some of the world's best dancers come together to dance their asses off. My sisters and I, like everyone else, have been practicing, rehearsing, and doing our very best to eat right so that this moment can be special for you all!"

The crowd cheered once again.

"This year, I didn't ask my family for presents. Normally, I would. Instead, this year, all I wanted was peace, my daughter Blessing to wear a smile on her face, and for my sisters to find happiness. We didn't do Thanksgiving this year, so I'm getting it all out now."

The crowd laughed, and as I looked out into the audience,

I could see my mother and father, Dru, Blessing, Blair, and of course, Dakota.

"As the season is coming to an end, my reason is sitting right there!" I pointed at my family, and I could hear the sniffles coming from my sisters behind me.

"Merry Christmas you all, now let's get this party started!"

The music started, I threw off my mic, and it was time to go to work! We decided to dance the Christmas show alone. I think we all realized that the perfect partners were our men, and we couldn't expect them to be doing all that moving around. Even though Dru wasn't my "man," he was still my man.

Everything eventually worked out for the best. In the new year, Blair and Holiday definitely got married. Their wedding was one for the books, but surprisingly, they didn't have any dancers. Blair said the best couldn't dance because the best were getting married—little cocky ass, and we were patiently waiting for my niece to be born. Silent and Dakota were also doing well—heavily dating. Silent said when she was with Dakota, it made her feel like she was floating on air.

Dru and I, we were taking it one day at a time, but I think it's also fair to say, I'm taken for life, because Dru isn't going anywhere, and neither am I...